'You mean you bought those tickets without asking?' Natalie said. 'Wow – are you going to be in trouble when your mom finds out!'

'Who says she's going to find out?' Cheryl said. 'I've got a plan that means she won't know a thing about it.'

'What kind of plan?' Amanda asked.

Cheryl grinned. 'I was kind of hoping you'd ask me that,' Cheryl said. 'Because you, Amanda Allen, are the very person who's going to make sure my brilliant plan comes off. If you want to go to the concert, that is.'

Uh-oh! I didn't like the sound of that. And I liked it even less when Amanda said, 'I'll do it! Whatever it is! I'll *do it*!'

Little Sister books published by Red Fox

Sneaking Out

Allan Frewin Jones

Series created by
Ben M. Baglio

RED FOX

A Red Fox Book

Published by Random House Children's Books
20 Vauxhall Bridge Road, London SW1V 2SA

A division of Random House UK Ltd
London Melbourne Sydney Auckland
Johannesburg and agencies throughout the world

1 3 5 7 9 10 8 6 4 2

First published in Great Britain by Red Fox 1995

Set in Plantin by Intype, London
Printed and bound in Great Britain
by Cox & Wyman Ltd, Reading, Berkshire

RANDOM HOUSE UK Limited Reg. No. 954009

ISBN 0 09 938421 3

Chapter One

You know what it's like. You open a magazine and this big movie star or rock star smiles out at you from the pool-side or from a beach in the Bahamas. Somewhere really sunny and hot and fabulous.

The writing under the photo always says something like: *Babs Morello takes time off from shooting her next blockbuster movie to relax at her Bermuda beach house.* Or, *Paulie Peters hangs out with fans before his next sell-out concert in San Francisco.*

And you look out of the window in Four Corners, Indiana, and the sky is grey, and you've got some really difficult homework to finish and hand in tomorrow or Ms Fenwick will go crazy. And baby Sam is crying; and no matter *how* much you love him, it's driving you nuts!

And these glamorous people smile up at you out of the magazine with their suntans and their perfect teeth. And you just have to do *something* to even things up a little.

So you take out a pen and draw a pair of glasses on the picture. You just can't help yourself. Who cares if it's a really childish thing to do? Who cares if you're ten years old and you're acting like you're *six*. And then you blank out a couple of front teeth and give Babs or Paulie a really dumb haircut. A bolt through the neck, like Frankenstein's monster, a couple of good scars and some stubble.

It is *so* satisfying to do that!

And that was all I was doing when my sister Amanda came in and started to scream.

I guess I'd better introduce myself before I start telling you about how I was chased all over the house by my crazy sister. And I'd better explain on whose picture I had drawn the glasses, missing teeth, curly moustache and cowboy hat.

My name's Stacy Allen. I live with my mom and dad in a quiet street in a small town right in the middle of Indiana. The house has gotten a little too small recently, due to the arrival last year of my baby brother Sam.

Sam was kind of a surprise all round. A *nice* surprise, but surprise all the same. It still amazes me how someone that small can kind of take over the whole house.

(I'm going to say this next bit really quietly. Mom hasn't mentioned it recently, and I don't want to remind her about it – but *things* have been said about sleeping arrangements once Sam starts getting bigger. Things like, 'Stacy and Amanda can share a room.' Have you heard the phrase, 'over my dead body'? *That*'s how I feel about that idea.)

There is one other person living in our house, and one cat. The cat is the nicest cat in the world. The person is my big, dumb, sister, Amanda.

Let me tell you about the nicest cat in the world first. He's around one and a half years old. I think you'd have to say he was cute rather than particularly intelligent – although he can be smart enough when it suits him. He's got a sleek grey coat and long black whiskers and he's called Benjamin. I got him as a present two Christmasses ago. He's a pedigree cat. A Russian Blue – and he's all *mine*!

Which leaves Amanda. She's thirteen but she thinks she's eighteen. She's your all-American blonde-haired cheerleader – all high kicks and high hair and 'Hi, guys, what's new?'

There are times when I feel I could murder

Amanda. And then there are other times when I think it's really great to have a sister like her. Like when she's performing out in front of the cheerleading squad, and I get this proud feeling, because she's *my* sister and she looks great. And she's a really talented artist. I mean, *really*! It's amazing. She talks about boys and clothes and hairdos and dumb stuff like that, and then she goes off and creates a beautiful painting, like, out of *nowhere*.

And then the next thing I know, she's yelling at me and calling me Metalmouth, and I'm yelling back and calling her a bimbo. (She calls me Metalmouth on account of my brace – I call her Bimbo because she can be a total airhead.)

Amanda has these crazes. Last year it was oil-paints. All of a sudden she wasn't interested in anything except painting in oils. Mom and Dad must have spent half a fortune getting her kitted out, and then, after about three months, she decided she wanted to work in clay. She didn't want to be a painter after all – she wanted to be a sculptor.

Then it was a few weeks of 'Dad, I need a kiln. Can I have a kiln, huh? Can I? I really need one.' A kiln is a special sort of oven where you bake clay. Talk about expensive! I'll tell you, it wasn't long before even Amanda realised there was no way Mom and Dad could afford a kiln. Which was lucky for them, because a couple of months later she was totally crazy about watercolours.

I'm just mentioning this, to give you an idea of how *fickle* Amanda can be. She's like it all the time.

And, of course, every time she finds something new to get excited about, everyone in the house – everyone in the street – everyone in the entire neighbourhood – gets to hear about it.

Take her current obsession with Eddie Eden. He's a rock star. At least, he's a rock star *now*. Last year he was one of the actors in *Spindrift*, our favourite daytime soap. You used to have to clean the drool off the TV set after Amanda had been watching him. And it's even worse now, because he's got a hit record and there are pictures of him in every magazine and newspaper you ever pick up.

We were told in school about these special satellites orbiting earth that send back these weird coloured pictures of the planet. I don't know how it works, except that it's something to do with the red splotches being areas where there's lots of people, and the blue stuff being deserts and oceans and so on. Now, if there was a special satellite up there, tuned in to pick up on photographs of Eddie Eden, then Amanda's bedroom would be the brightest red spot in the whole U.S.A.

I like Eddie Eden's music – but I can't understand why Amanda thinks he's so gorgeous. All he's got is this thick black hair and these bright blue eyes. Oh, and a really cute smile. And I guess he dances well and he's in pretty good shape, if you like that hunky kind of thing.

Oh, OK! I'll admit it – I think he's pretty good-looking, too. I just don't want Amanda to know. It's a whole lot more fun driving her crazy by pretending I think he's a total loser than it would be just to go along with her.

A little sister has to have her fun somehow! You'd feel the same if *you* had a big sister like Amanda.

Anyway, back to the Stacy-ised picture in the magazine.

Eddie Eden's big smile looked really funny with a few of the front teeth blacked out. And I'd also discovered that, if I blacked out the whites of his eyes on either side of his nose, he looked cross-eyed.

I was giggling away to myself as I gave him

a nice big curly moustache and a pair of spectacles like Mrs Lloyd next door wears. You know – the kind with *wings* sticking out of the sides.

That was when Amanda came into the kitchen.

'Stacy!' she yelled. 'I wanted that picture.'

I nearly jumped out of my chair. I'd been concentrating so hard on customising Eddie Eden's photo that I hadn't even noticed she was breathing down my neck until she nearly deafened me by yelling right in my ear.

I've got to admit, I felt pretty embarrassed. I mean, drawing silly faces on photographs isn't exactly the most grown-up thing to be caught doing.

'Don't sneak up on me like that!' I said. 'You've already got twenty-three million pictures of Eddie Eden.'

'I don't have *that* picture!' Amanda said. 'I asked Mom to save that magazine for me. I asked her *especially*!'

'No one told me anything about it,' I said. 'Anyway – it's an improvement. In fact, if you want me to, I can go up to your room right now and make some improvements to all the others.'

'You're a rat, Stacy Allen,' Amanda said.

11

'Just you wait until there's something important to you! Just you wait!'

She turned and walked out of the kitchen. I heard her run upstairs and slam her bedroom door.

As fights between Amanda and I go, that was pretty tame. Usually, Amanda is a whole lot more feisty than that.

I knew *why* she wasn't feeling up to having a real yelling-match with me. It had to do with Eddie Eden.

You see, Eddie Eden was on tour right then. He was taking his show clear across America. It was called the "This Way to Paradise" tour, and he was playing a couple of nights really close to where we live. One concert was actually going to be in Four Corners, and the other in Mayville, which is only a few miles away.

I guess you're wondering why that should be a problem.

The problem was that the theatre in Four Corners is way over on the far side of town and Mom and Dad said Amanda couldn't go. They said she was too young to go to a rock concert.

(Mom said, 'Maybe, next year, honey.' Next *year*? I don't believe the way parents sometimes come out with stuff like that. Next *year*

12

– like it's only just around the corner. What kind of a person can wait an entire year for something? Even *I* could sympathise with Amanda on that one.)

Amanda had been kind of down about it for the last few weeks. She'd tried to talk them into letting her go. She'd tried bargaining with them – you know. 'If I get a B+ for my science project, can I go to the concert?' She'd even tried convincing them that she'd be *ill* if she couldn't go. But nothing worked. She wasn't going to the concert, and that was that.

I hadn't doodled over that picture of Eddie Eden to upset her all over again. I didn't know she wanted it. She really has got pictures of him all over her room. You'd think one more or less wouldn't matter.

I tried de-customising the picture with an eraser, but all I managed to do was to rub a hole clean through the page – taking Eddie's top front tooth with it.

Now I'm not always in line for a 'Sister of the Year' award, but I was feeling kind of sorry for Amanda – as well as feeling a little guilty that I hadn't apologised for messing up her picture. And this was one time when I could actually do something to put things right – at least as far as the photograph was concerned.

I called down to the basement, where Mom has her office. 'Mom, I'm just going out for ten minutes.'

'OK, honey,' Mom called back.

Mom works as a manuscript proofreader for books that haven't been published yet. She's got a proper little office down in our basement, with a word processor and everything. Proof-reading is the kind of job that can be done from home, which means she can be around for Sam and us and earn money at the same time. Which is kind of useful when there's not a whole lot of spare cash around, what with diapers and toys for Sam, paints and brushes for Amanda and my monthly mail-order wild-life books.

I went down to the store and bought another copy of the magazine with that picture of Eddie Eden in it.

I bought a candy bar, too. After all, doing a good deed for Amanda, I figured that I ought to get *some* kind of reward.

Back home, I went upstairs and knocked on Amanda's bedroom door.

'Amanda? It's me-ee! Your favourite sister. I've got something for you,' I called.

'Go away,' Amanda said through the closed door. 'I'm not talking to you.'

'You will be when you see what I've got,' I said.

I folded the magazine open to the page with the photo of Eddie Eden.

Amanda snatched the door open. 'Why don't you just . . . oh!' She stood blinking at the photo. 'Oh . . . you cleaned it all off.'

I grinned at her. 'Who's a rat, Amanda? Am I still a rat, huh?'

She smiled. 'No, you're not a rat,' she said.

'So are you going to cut it out and put it up?' I asked. 'Or are you planning on keeping it under your pillow with those buttons and postcards?'

'I do not keep buttons and postcards under my pillow,' Amanda said. She grinned. 'Well – only *one* postcard.'

I went into her room. Gee! Talk about a *shrine* to Eddie Eden. There were posters and double-page spreads from magazines. There were black-and-white newspaper pictures and coloured pictures cut out of TV guides. And on one wall she had pinned up a whole bunch of her own drawings of him – taken from pictures. I was surprised she even had room for another picture – unless she was planning on glueing it to the ceiling!

I sat on her bed while she cut the picture out.

I've got to admit, I was feeling pretty good about myself. *Come on down, Stacy Allen: selfless sister of the semester*! Of course, this good deed also meant Amanda *owed* me one – which is always a good position to be in. Amanda could do me a favour sometime.

But it wasn't long before I found out that it wasn't Amanda who was going to be doing me a big favour in the near future. It was going to be the other way around entirely!

And it all had to do with Eddie Eden again. Although, before that happened, there was plenty of excitement to come, courtesy of my friend, Fern Kipsak.

Chapter Two

I'd just arrived home from school and I was trying to decide whether I felt like having some chocolate and hazelnut spread on toast, or whether I'd prefer a few fresh-baked brownies, when the phone rang.

It was Fern.

'Come over right away,' she said, sounding excited.

'Why? What's up?' I asked. What *could* be up? I mean, I was *with* her half an hour earlier.

'It's a surprise,' Fern said. 'And it's a secret, too – so don't go blabbing to anyone.'

'Blabbing about *what*?' I asked. 'You haven't told me anything yet. What's going on?'

'My house, twenty minutes,' Fern said.

That was pretty typical of Fern.

Fern Kipsak is one of my three best friends. The other two are Pippa Kane and Cindy Spiegel. Cindy is my absolute best friend ever, but Fern and Pippa come pretty close, and we do a whole heap of stuff together.

Fern gets a little *hyper* sometimes. She's the smallest of us four, but she makes up for it by being the loudest.

I checked with Mom that it was OK to go over to Fern's house, then set off. Sometimes I ride my bike over there, but it was a nice, bright afternoon, so I decided to walk. It only takes about fifteen minutes.

When I arrived at Fern's house, Pippa was waiting outside. She led me round the side of the house to the toolshed.

'What's going on?' I asked Pippa. 'What's the big secret?'

'You'll see,' Pippa said. 'It's completely phenomenal!'

Pippa does tend to talk like that. She's the brains of the gang, I guess. She *knows* lots of things – things that normal people forget. Like the capital of Montana or the date of the first manned moon-landing. Just don't ever ask Pippa to do anything practical – and don't *ever* take her advice. That always leads to trouble.

Anyway, I headed around to the toolshed with Pippa. She gave a strange knock on the door. Tap, tap-tap. Tap-tap-tap. Tap.

'What are you doing?' I asked.

'Secret knock,' Pippa said mysteriously.

'Huh?' *Secret knock?*

The four of us might be a gang, but we weren't the sort of gang that has a clubhouse and secret knocks. We used to have a code for sending one another secret messages, but the problem with that was that Pippa had invented the code, and it was so complicated that she was the only person who could remember it.

Which meant that if Cindy sent me a coded message saying *DMMP DM HRPOEQM OSGHHB WP PGNMM PGENPX*, I had to go and find Pippa before I could figure out that it said: *Meet me outside school at three-thirty*. And by the time I'd found Pippa and had it translated, Cindy would have gotten fed up waiting for me, and gone home. Which explains why we don't do things like that any more. But it doesn't explain why Pippa was doing a secret knock on Fern's toolshed door.

The toolshed door opened and Cindy's face appeared.

'Come on in, quick,' she said.

It took me a few seconds to get used to the gloom in there. The only light came in through a grimy window in the back wall. The tool shed was full of all the usual garden junk. Broken mower, rusty spades and shears, a couple of sad-looking lawn chairs and a filthy old barbecue.

Fern was crouched in one corner with her back to me.

'Oh, *wow*!' I said, going over to her. There were some blankets piled in the corner, and, lying on the blankets with its head on Fern's knees, was a dog.

It was what my dad calls a *mixed-salad* dog. A mongrel. It was sort of small with a long muzzle and floppy ears and big brown eyes. It was mostly white, but with flecks and patches of black and brown all over.

'Where did you find it?' I asked, kneeling down beside Fern and giving the dog's head a stroke. It looked up at me with its big brown eyes and I went kind of gooey inside. A little like I do when Sam reaches out and grabs my fingers in his fist. (I go a lot *gooier* with Sam, but you know what I mean.)

'She was whimpering at the back door,' Fern said. 'I think there's something wrong with her. She's really affectionate.'

'We're going to call her Hobo,' Cindy said.

'I still think we should call her Lafayette,' Pippa said. 'Lafayette's a much nicer name for a lady dog.'

'I found her,' Fern said. 'So I get to pick her name. And she's going to be called Hobo.'

'Are you *keeping* her?' I asked.

Fern looked uncertainly at me. 'I hope so,' she said. 'I've got to sell the idea to my folks first. That's why I wanted you all to come over. I need plenty of good reasons why we should have a dog.'

Pippa and Cindy came and knelt beside Hobo and we all petted her.

'She's kind of tubby,' said Pippa. 'Wherever she comes from, they haven't been starving her.' Pippa was right. Now I looked, Hobo was very stout around the middle.

'So if she comes from such a good home, how come she was outside our back door, whining and scratching to be let in?' Fern said.

'She must be lost,' said Pippa. 'You never know – there might be a reward for finding her.'

'I don't want a reward,' Fern said. 'I want to keep her. Look, she doesn't have a collar or anything. If you ask me, she's just a stray. Look at her coat – she hasn't been brushed or had a bath for ages. Come on, guys, help me think up some good reasons to use on my folks so I can keep her.'

'She's really fat,' said Pippa, stroking

Hobo's bulging tummy. 'Oh my gosh!' she said suddenly.

'What?' Fern asked. Pippa was kneeling up with her hands over her mouth and nose.

'Oh my gosh!' she said again.

'What?' we all chorused.

'She's not *fat*,' Pippa said. 'She's . . . she's *thingy*! You know – *thingy*! She's going to be a *mom*! She's got a tummy full of puppies!'

We all gazed down at Hobo. She lifted her head and gave a little whine, as if to say, 'That's right, I am one heavily pregnant dog.'

'Oh, crumbs,' Fern said. 'What do we do?' She looked around at us. 'I don't know how to do all the things you have to when a dog's going to have puppies.'

'You can't keep her in the shed,' Cindy said. 'It'll be too cold. She needs to be somewhere warm.' She looked at Fern. 'Do you think your folks would let you take her in?'

'I don't know,' Fern said. 'I wasn't even sure if they'd go for a dog at all. That's why I wanted some good reasons from you guys. But a *pregnant* dog . . .' She shook her head.

'I think you'd better find out pretty quickly,' Pippa said. 'I don't think Hobo's going to be able to wait around much longer.'

Fern stood up. 'OK,' she said. 'You guys

wait here. I'll go and get my mom. And for heaven's sake – think up some good reasons why Hobo needs to stay with us.'

We kneeled and petted Hobo.

'Fern's mom will be OK about it,' I said, stroking Hobo's head. 'I'm sure she will be.'

★ ★ ★

I couldn't wait to tell everyone about Hobo when I got home later that afternoon.

'And Fern wants to make a video of the puppies being born,' I said.

'Ew! Gross!' Amanda said, squirming on the couch. 'That is just so disgusting!'

'No it's not!' I said. 'It's educational. Fern is thinking of renting out the video to the school for biology class.'

'So Fern's mom is going to let her keep the dog?' asked Dad.

'I guess so,' I said. 'She said we should put up notices in the neighborhood. You know – "Mongrel dog found". And a description of her. Just in case anyone's looking for her. But Fern's mom doesn't think anyone will get in touch. She thinks whoever owned the dog just dumped her when they found out she was expecting puppies.'

'People who do things like that shouldn't be

allowed to have pets,' Amanda said. 'That's just so cruel!'

'And what plans do they have over there for the pups?' Mom asked. 'Surely they're not planning to keep them all?'

'Fern's going to put a notice in the store,' I said. Oh, I forgot to mention, Fern's mom and dad run a general store – you know, the kind of place that stays open until really late and sells everything from strawberry milkshakes to house-plants.

The first thing we'd done that afternoon, once Mrs Kipsak had agreed that Fern should keep Hobo (at least temporarily), was to run down to the store and get a good supply of dog food, as well as food and drinking bowls and some toys.

'How many puppies do you think there will be?' I asked.

'Anything between about five and eight, usually,' Mom said. 'And they're going to advertise for homes for them?'

'Yeah,' I said thoughtfully. 'Mom . . .?'

'Forget it,' Mom said.

I frowned at her. 'You don't even know what I was going to say.'

'I'm sorry,' Mom said. 'I thought you were going to ask whether we could take one of the puppies. I thought I'd save you the trouble of asking, because there's no way we're going to have a puppy. They take too much looking after. Anyway – what *were* you going to say, Stacy?'

'Nothing,' I said.

'Hmmm,' Mom said.

Of course, she knew I'd been about to ask whether we could have one of Hobo's puppies. And I knew she knew. And she knew I knew she knew.

'I bet you end up getting a puppy,' Amanda said. 'Some people in this house *always* get what they want.' She folded her arms in a real huffy way. 'And *some* people don't get *anything* they want at all. No matter *how* much it means to them.'

Mom and Dad looked at each other.

'For the last time,' Mom said. 'You're too young to go all the way across town to a concert that doesn't end until eleven o'clock at night.'

Amanda gave her a surprised look. 'Concert?' she said. 'Did I mention anything about a concert? I don't think so. I don't think the name Eddie Eden even passed my lips. All I was saying was that some people get things all

25

their own way, and some people don't. That's all I was saying.'

'I don't get things all my own way,' I said.

'Not if it involves a puppy, that's for sure,' Mom said.

'Yeah, well,' Amanda said, standing up. 'I think I'll just go on up to my room and listen to some music.' She gave us all a real good frown as she stood at the door. 'And I guess I'd better make the most of it, seeing as it's the *closest* I'm ever going to *get* to the real thing.'

She stamped upstairs.

'She's not going to give up,' Dad said. 'Don't you think we should – ' Mom interrupted him with a really loud cough.

I wondered what Dad had been about to say. Maybe he thought Amanda should be allowed to go to the concert, but Mom had put her foot down about it.

Mom does tend to make all the big day-to-day decisions. Mainly because she's *here* and Dad spends a lot of time out at work.

He works as a book salesman – selling books to stores. He works mostly up in the north-west corner of the state and across the state-line in Chicago. It means that sometimes he doesn't get home until way after my bedtime.

It also means that sometimes he's away from home for a few days, which is no fun at all.

I looked at Dad. 'Do you like puppies?' I asked. I was thinking that maybe if I could get Dad on my side, then we might be able to bring Mom around between us.

'Sure I do,' Dad said. 'But your mom's right – we can't have a puppy, sweetheart. Who'd look after it?'

'*I* would,' I said.

'And who'd have to take over when you were at school?' Mom said. 'Listen, Stacy, dogs aren't like cats. Dogs take a whole lot more looking after. It's really not a good idea, honey.'

'OK,' I said with a sigh. 'I guess not.'

'And what do you think Benjamin would make of it?' Dad asked.

Dad had a good point there. What *would* Benjamin make of a puppy in *his* house? Puppy-burgers, probably, judging by the way he hisses at the Lloyds' terrier over the back fence.

Oh, well, it was a nice dream. *At least I'd get to play with the puppies over at Fern's house before they went off to their new homes*, I thought.

The one thing none of us knew right then was how soon Hobo was going to give birth. But she didn't keep us guessing for long.

Chapter Three

Breakfast the next morning was the usual chaos. Sam was in his high chair at the table. Mom has started letting him feed himself. She says it's good practice for him. And he sure needed the practice, because right then he was trying to feed himself by pushing oatmeal up his nose.

I was finishing a letter to my pen pal. I'd been writing to him for a while. His name's Craig Newman and he lives in Pennsylvania.

Dad was eating with one hand and going through some papers with the other. Mom was fixing lunch for Amanda and me. The portable TV was talking away to itself in the corner, and Benjamin was cruising around Sam's high chair, licking up blobs of fallen oatmeal.

Mom looked at the clock.

'Give Amanda another call, honey,' she said to me.

Amanda isn't always too good at dragging herself out of bed in the morning. What she needs is my patented *Cat Alarm*.

Yes, folks, here it is, the genuine, all-fur, satisfaction guaranteed Benjomatic Cat Alarm! No batteries, no fuss. Just place the Benjomatic Cat Alarm on your bed last thing at night and you need never worry about oversleeping again.

The Benjomatic Cat Alarm's breakthrough features include:

1. *A wet nose in the ear*
2. *A brain-rattling purr*
3. *A great heavy body that will sit on your chest until you get up and open a tin of cat food.*

Of course, as Amanda doesn't much like cats, and never lets Benjamin set a paw inside her room, I don't suppose she'd be too pleased at being woken up with a wet nose, a loud purr and a heavy weight on her.

I went out into the hall and was about to give Amanda a yell when I had a better idea. I opened the front door very quietly and rang the bell. Then I closed the door quietly again and made stamping noises as if I'd just walked into the hall. I pulled the door open.

'Oh, hi, Cheryl,' I said loudly. 'No, I'm afraid she's not up yet. Oh, OK, I'll tell her you couldn't wait.'

Ha! That did the trick. There was a stampede of feet along the upstairs hallway as Amanda zipped into the bathroom.

'Cheryl!' she yelled. 'I'm coming. Wait a minute.'

I went back into the kitchen.

'There you go,' I told Mom. 'Amanda's up.'

'Cute trick,' Dad said. 'You're getting so sharp you'll have to be careful you don't cut yourself.'

Three minutes later, Amanda came bursting breathlessly into the kitchen.

'Where is she?' she panted, showing all the signs of having got herself washed and dressed in record time. 'Didn't she *wait*?'

'Sit down and eat your breakfast,' Mom said. 'Cheryl was never here.'

'You!' Amanda hollered, glaring at me.

I grinned at her and nodded. 'Me. Smart, huh?'

'Stacy, has anyone told you, you're –' Amanda's head snapped around towards the TV. '*Waaah*! Shut up everyone!'

I hadn't heard it, but then Amanda is kind

31

of tuned into certain things. Like the name Eddie Eden being mentioned.

(You could walk three blocks away and whisper 'Eddie Eden', and I swear Amanda's ears would pick it up.)

Amanda was hopping from foot to foot. We all looked at the TV. It was a local report. A woman called Mariel Snood who does the celebrity stuff in our area. She was interviewing Eddie Eden.

He was lounging in a big armchair in jeans and a flashy white shirt unbuttoned to show his chest.

'Hi, Eddie,' Mariel said. 'It's a real pleasure to meet you. And what brings you into our studios today?'

'Oh, you know,' Eddie said, 'I'm doing some promo work for my tour.' He smiled into the camera. 'I hope you folks will come and see me.'

Amanda made a groaning noise.

'That's great,' Mariel said. 'Eddie? Would you be prepared to do us a *bi-ig* favour? I know you're not expecting this . . .' She grinned into the camera. 'But would you be prepared to take some calls from our viewers?'

'Sure thing,' said Eddie.

'What a fake!' I said. 'Of course he knew

about it. He's sitting there with the phone right next to him!'

'What's the number? What's the number?' Amanda moaned to herself.

'If you'd like to speak to Eddie Eden,' Mariel said, 'the number to call is . . .'

Amanda bounded out into the hall and pounced on the phone like a cat on a mouse.

'And while we're waiting for that first call,' Mariel said, 'I'll just take time out to remind you that Eddie will be signing copies of his new record in Rocky's Record Store on the third floor of the Clearwater Mall in uptown Springfield between three and five-thirty this afternoon.'

'What did she say?' Amanda yelled from the doorway, getting herself all tangled up in the phone cord as she spun around to look at the TV.

'He's going to be making a personal appearance in the mall,' Mom said. 'To sign records. Amanda, don't yell like that!'

'I've got to go there!' Amanda howled. 'What time did they say?'

'Between three and five-thirty,' Dad said, stepping over the phone cord as Amanda came walking across the kitchen floor like she was hypnotised by the TV.

She stared at the phone. 'What?' she said. 'You're kidding!' She looked at the TV. Eddie was on the phone, answering a question about his favourite flavour of ice-cream.

'What did they say?' I asked, getting kind of caught up in Amanda's enthusiasm. 'I want to ask a question, too.'

'Help yourself,' Amanda said, reaching out the receiver toward me without taking her eyes off the TV screen.

I held the receiver to my ear. A prerecorded voice spoke: 'You are on hold. Your call will be answered in rotation. Waiting time is eleven minutes and twenty seconds. Thank you for calling.'

'I'm leaving now,' Dad said from the hall. 'If anyone wants a lift to school, they'd better get moving.'

'I'll take the bus,' Amanda called. 'I want to – *what*?'

'That's all we've got time for right now,' Mariel said. 'I'd like to thank Eddie Eden for coming on our program, and now I'll hand you over to Mark Rothwell for the latest sports round-up.'

'Arrgh!' Amanda hollered. 'He only took two calls.' Eddie vanished off the TV and was replaced by a bunch of guys playing football.

'What kind of a two-bit TV channel is this? Who cares about some dumb game of football?'

Sam started crying and whacking his spoon on his tray. Blobs of oatmeal sprayed everywhere. It was a good job we had Benjamin to vacuum it all up. Cats are very useful for cleaning spilled food off the floor. Benjamin does a really good job on plates, too, although you have to give them to him when Mom isn't looking!

'Now look what you've done,' Mom said, picking Sam up and giving him a cuddle. 'There, there, baby. Did your horrid big sister frighten you with all her yelling. Don't you worry about it.' She looked at Amanda. 'Big sister is going to school now, where she can do all the yelling she likes without scaring you half to death.'

'Does anyone want a lift?' Dad asked.

'Me!' I said, running up to my room to get my school bag.

'I'm going to see Eddie Eden!' Amanda sang, grabbing Mom, squashing Sam and dancing them around the floor. 'I'm going to see Eddie Eden this afternoon!'

'You and about four thousand others,' Mom

said. 'Amanda – be careful, honey. You'll make him dizzy.'

Amanda let go of Mom and Sam and ran up to her room. We nearly collided in the hallway as she came dancing out, waving her bag in the air.

'Edd-EE! Edd-EE!' she chanted. 'Oh! If only I'd known sooner! I could have gotten the squad together. We could have made up a special cheer for him.' She went sailing down the banisters and landed in front of Dad.

'E is for *exciting*!' she shouted, going into one of her bounce, jump, squat, wave-your-arms-around routines. 'D is for *delirious*! D is also for . . . for . . .'

'Dopey!' I said, walking down the stairs.

'Mnyaah!' Amanda stuck her tongue out.

Dad opened the front door and Mom came out into the hallway, carrying Sam.

'I'm going to be late back,' Amanda shouted to Mom. 'I'm going to be at the mall right after school!'

'Hey, wait a minute,' Mom called. 'Haven't you already told me you were going to be late today?'

'No,' Amanda said. 'I only just found out!'

Mom came out to the car. 'Amanda, honey

– you *did* say you'd be late this afternoon. Think about it. You told me last week.'

Ding! It suddenly dawned on me. Last Friday. I was watching TV and Amanda was going on about wanting her cheerleader uniform washed – because she was leading the squad at a basketball game one afternoon. One afternoon *this* week. Or, to be more precise, *this* afternoon.

'*Nooooo*!' Amanda howled. 'This isn't happening to me! This *can't* be happening to me. And it's an *away* game. I'll be clear over on the wrong side of town!' She gave Mom a panicky look. 'They'll let me off. They'll let me off the squad for one afternoon, won't they? Yeah, sure they will. No problem. Cheryl can lead them. Or Natalie. Yeah – ' She slumped into the back of the car. 'Phee-eww! I'll get out of it somehow. Sheesh! Why does it always happen to *me*?'

'Hey,' I said, shoving in beside her as Dad started the car. 'Don't *say* that, Amanda. You *deserve* it!'

I grinned at her. 'You should have seen your face when you thought you might miss Eddie Eden! I wish I'd had a camera!'

Amanda wrapped her arms around her head

and sank into the back seat as Dad steered the car down the driveway and out into the street.

'Eddie Eden!' she sighed. 'In the flesh!'

Dad laughed.

It looked like all Amanda's months of adoring Eddie Eden from afar were finally going to pay off. I could see it now – at three o'clock exactly, straight after school, there would be one face in particular pressed up against the glass doors of Rocky's Record Store.

Eddie Eden's number one fan – Amanda Allen, drool-leader and swoon queen of Four Corners Middle School.

Well, rather her than me. I had no intention of being crushed to death by twenty thousand half-crazed Eddie Eden fans. No way.

Chapter Four

I met up with Cindy and Pippa by the lockers. They were completely engrossed in a book Pippa was holding.

'You see?' Pippa said. 'If you use the whelping table, you can figure out exactly when the pups are going to be born.'

'What's *whelping*?' Cindy asked.

'It means giving birth,' Pippa said. 'Isn't that *obvious*?'

'Not to me,' Cindy said. 'It could have meant anything.'

'Hi, guys,' I said. 'What are you reading?'

'Stacy!' Cindy said. 'Look at this, Pippa found a book all about dogs. It's got a chapter on pregnancy and whelping.'

'Oh, right,' I said. 'I thought I heard you say something about a whelping table. Let me look. What does one look like? Is it a special kind of table that vets use?'

Pippa pointed to a page full of numbers in a kind of grid.

'A whelping table isn't *furniture*,' she said. 'It's a graph to help you figure out when the pups are due. You see? The mom dog is pregnant for sixty-three days on average. So all you need to know is when the mom and dad got together, and then you can work out exactly when the pups are due. Neat, huh?'

'Great,' I said. 'So have you *asked* Hobo when it happened?'

Pippa stared at me for a moment then gave a silly grin. 'I guess it's not all that useful after all,' she said. She turned the page. 'But there's other stuff that *will* be useful. Stuff about what to do when the puppies are due.'

'Hi, everyone.' It was Fern.

'How's Hobo?' Cindy asked. 'Pippa's got a book about dogs.'

'Oh, good,' Fern said. 'Let me take a look at that.'

'Just a *minute*,' Pippa said as Fern tried to grab the book out of her hands. 'Excuse me, but this is *my* book. Tell me what you want to know, and I'll look it up for you.' Pippa likes to be in control.

'I want to know how much we should be

40

feeding Hobo,' Fern said. 'She doesn't seem to want to each much.'

'OK,' Pippa said in her professor voice. 'Feeding of pregnant dog. I'll look that up in the index.'

'Have you fixed her a bed yet?' I asked.

'She kind of chose that for herself,' Fern said. 'She was curling up in the bottom of the clothes closet in the hall. So Mom said we may as well make that her official bedroom. We've put a box in there with an old blanket in it. She's really cosy in there.'

'Here we are,' Pippa said. 'Diet during pregnancy.' She ran her finger down the page. ' "In the first three weeks you should keep to a normal balanced diet. From four to nine weeks the dog will require a higher food intake, especially of protein. As the pregnancy progresses the dog will become extremely hungry and should be fed three times a day." ' She looked at Fern. 'Are you feeding her three times a day?'

'She's not eating very much,' Fern said. 'I told you that. Oh, heck! Maybe there's something wrong with her.'

'She's got to eat,' Cindy said. 'Maybe she just doesn't like what you're giving her? Maybe she's used to a particular sort of food.'

'Like what?' Fern asked.

'I heard of a cat once that wouldn't eat anything other than tuna fish,' I said.

'You think I should try Hobo on *tuna fish*?' Fern said.

'No. I didn't mean that. I was just agreeing with Cindy. Maybe Hobo only likes one kind of food.'

'You'll have to give her samples of a whole lot of different stuff,' Pippa said. 'That's the only way to find out what she likes.'

The bell sounded for the start of school and we made our way to homeroom.

Fern and Pippa were arguing over who should look after the book. Fern said *she* should because it was *her* dog that was expecting the puppies. Pippa said *she* should, because she'd be able to explain all the technical stuff, and because it was *her* book.

In the end we worked out a system. Fern would get to keep the book until lunch break, and then Pippa would take over. The next morning I would get to read the book, and Cindy would have it in the afternoon, after me.

During the morning Fern kept slipping us notes under the desk. I kept one eye on Ms Fenwick as I opened the slip of paper in my lap. Ms Fenwick has got eyes like a hawk, so you have to be extra-careful with her if you want to pass each other messages.

Teachers don't always realise that there are some things you have to tell your friends *right away*.

I did my best to look like I was paying attention while I tried to read Fern's note under the desk.

Plany for obith, I read. I gave Fern a puzzled look. Fern's writing is out of this world. I tried the next line.

A) soap, disengested and a snail had basin. What the heck was Fern writing about? I couldn't make out the next word at all, although I thought it might start with a "C". OK. *C-something. Old tonsils. Shoon. Sick or baited cotton. Clean new pups.*

I didn't get Fern's note translated until the end of the lesson.

'What the heck was all that?' I asked her. 'Old tonsils?'

'Old towels,' said Fern. 'Can't you read?'

'Sure I can read,' I told her. 'If a person can *write*.'

'Give me that note.' Fern said. 'It's clear as day, Stacy. "Planning for a birth. A) Soap, disinfectant and a small hand basin".'

43

'I thought that said "a snail had basin",' I told her.

'A snail had basin?' Fern said. 'What the heck is that supposed to mean?'

'It means Fern's got the worst handwriting in the entire school,' Pippa said.

'So what does the next part say?' I asked.

'Cotton wool. Old towels. Scissors. Silk or boiled cotton. Clean newspaper.'

'That doesn't say "*newspaper*",' Cindy said. 'That says "*new pups*".'

'Oh, forget it,' Fern said. 'I'll just tell you from now on.' She thumbed through the book. 'I was reading this part about behaviour at whelping time. It says the dog will get restless and scratch up her bedding. The thing is, Hobo was like that last night. And she was whimpering. And it says she'll refuse food.' Fern looked at us. 'Didn't I tell you that Hobo wouldn't eat anything?'

'You mean she's already in labour?' Pippa said.

'That's what it says here,' Fern said.

'You mean she's probably having her pups right now?' Cindy said.

'Not necessarily,' Pippa said. 'It says the first stage of labour can go on for twenty-four hours.' She looked around at us. 'Hobo might have her pups tonight.'

'Oh, wow,' Cindy said. 'Do you think your mom would let us sleep over?'

'On a weekday?' Pippa said. 'I don't think my mom would let me.'

'No problem,' Fern said. 'I'll video the whole thing for you.'

'Can we name the puppies?' I asked.

'We could each choose two names,' Pippa said in her usual organising way. 'Then we put the names in a box and pick them out at random. That's the fairest way of doing it.'

I didn't really pay much attention in class for the rest of that morning. I was too busy trying to come up with good dog names. I got it down to a list of eight:

Boy dog names: King. Bruno. Thor. Hawkeye.
Girl dog names: Queenie. Bella. Princess. Rosemary.

I was still trying to whittle it down to my two favourite names as I made my way to the cafeteria for lunch.

'Stacy!' I looked around. Amanda was racing up the stairs, red-faced and looking as though she'd just been told the world was going to end in ten minutes.

'What name do you like better?' I asked her. 'Hawkeye or King?'

'What?' She came to a panting stop on the stairs.

'I'm trying to come up with some names for Hobo's puppies,' I said. 'And don't suggest Eddie.'

'Forget about that,' Amanda said. 'Stacy, you've got to help me. I'm in big trouble. You've really got to help me.'

'What's wrong?' I asked.

'I can't get out of heading the cheerleading squad this afternoon,' Amanda said. She scowled down the stairs. 'That's the last time I tell the truth to a teacher,' she said. 'I should have lied to her. I should have said I had to go to the dentist or had stomach ache.'

'So what happened?' I asked.

'I was *honest*,' Amanda said. 'I told Ms Shirley that I had to be at the mall between three and five-thirty this afternoon. I asked her if someone else could lead the squad just this once. And she said, "What's the problem?" And I said, "Eddie Eden is appearing at Rocky's Record Store." And do you know what Ms Shirley said?'

'No. What?' I asked, although I had a sneaky suspicion.

46

'She said, "Who is Eddie Eden?" ' Amanda stared at me. 'Like, she's never even *heard* of him.' (Hey! My sneaky suspicion was right!) 'So I started explaining who he was. And she said, "Oh, he's some *pop* star, is he?" *Some* pop star! I mean, come on – where do teachers live – under a rock or something?'

'I'm getting kind of hungry, Amanda,' I said. 'Are you *going* anywhere with this?'

'Stacy,' Amanda said, grabbing my arm. 'You've got to help me. Ms Shirley won't let me go to the mall. She says that if I don't lead the squad this afternoon, she'll take it as proof that I don't take the responsibility of the head cheerleader's job seriously. Don't you get it?' Amanda stared at me. 'If I go to the signing, Ms Shirley will pick someone else as squad leader.'

'That's bad luck, Amanda,' I said. 'But I don't see what I can do about it.' I shrugged. 'I'd help you if I could. But what can I do?'

You know. I really should learn to keep my mouth shut. There are times when a simple-sounding question like that can get you into a whole lot of trouble. Especially when Amanda is involved.

Chapter Five

'You could go for me,' Amanda said.

'You don't think Ms Shirley will notice the difference?' I said. 'We don't look too similar, Amanda.'

In fact, we look totally different. Amanda's got wavy blonde hair and a big smile. I've got straight brown hair and a big heap of freckles.

'I don't mean go to the basketball game for me!' Amanda said. 'I meant go to the mall. Get Eddie Eden to sign my copy of his CD.'

'Let me get this clear,' I said. 'You want me to go over to the mall this afternoon?'

'Yes.'

'Fight my way through hundreds of fans?'

'Yes!'

'And ask Eddie Eden to sign your CD?'

'*Yes*!'

'That's all?' I said. 'That's all you want me to do? You don't want me to invite him home for dinner, or anything?'

'He won't be able to – ' Amanda stopped. 'Oh! Ha, ha, Stacy. Big joke!'

'Maybe I could kidnap him for you?' I said. 'I mean, once I've fought my way through to him, it seems a shame to quit with only a measly autograph.'

'Will you *do* it?' Amanda asked. 'I'll be really grateful. And it's not much to ask.'

'Yes, it is,' I said. 'I could end up getting stomped on and squished and mashed and mangled. I've seen on TV what it's like at these signings. People come out the other end looking like they've been in a car crash.'

'You won't,' Amanda said. 'Trust me. Eddie Eden fans aren't like that. And if you do this little tiny, weeny thing for me, I'll be on your side about the puppy. I'll help you talk Mom into letting you have one of the puppies. How's that?'

'OK,' I said. 'It's a deal.'

I'd kind of given up on the puppy idea, but if Amanda was going to help, then maybe Mom could be talked round. But the best part of the deal was that I would have gone to the mall for Amanda anyway. I was just stringing her along a little. It doesn't pay to give in to Amanda's requests too quickly. Amanda's needs have a tendency to snowball if a person is too willing.

I met up with the others in the cafeteria. They were already over at our favourite table.

'Have you come up with any puppy names?' Cindy asked, as I took my tray over and sat down with them.

I showed them my list of names.

'Talk about tame,' Fern said. She pushed a piece of paper over to me. 'Now, *those* are good dog names!'

Ripper. Fang. Quasimodo. Rocky. Crusher. Spike.

'Quasimodo?' I said.

'Don't you know who Quasimodo is?' Fern said. 'He's the hunchback of Notre Dame. Haven't you seen the movie?' She went into a crook-backed crouch and shuffled around shouting, 'The bells. The *bells*!'

I didn't have the faintest idea what she was talking about. There was nothing strange about that; not where Fern was concerned.

Fern straightened up. 'What do you think of my other names, huh?' she asked.

'They're *different*,' I said. I looked at the others. 'What have you two come up with?'

Pippa read her list. 'Lafayette,' she began.

Fern groaned, but Pippa carried on. 'Laverne. Lulu. Caesar. Rupert. Mozart.'

'*Mozart*?' Fern said. 'What kind of a name is that for a dog?'

Pippa gave Fern one of her superior looks. 'For your information,' she said. 'Mozart was a great composer. There was a program on TV about him last week. He was the greatest composer in the world, but he died in total poverty.'

'Gee,' Fern said. 'And I didn't even know he was ill.'

'I think it's a great name for a dog,' Pippa said.

'Oh, sure,' Fern said. 'I can just see myself taking him for a walk in Maynard Park. "Here, Mozart! Good boy, Mozart! Fetch the stick, Mozart!" ' She looked at Cindy. 'You've got to come up with something better than that.' she said.

'Well,' Cindy began, 'I was thinking that the girls could be called something like Angel, or Susie or Moppet, or Mitten . . .'

Fern interrupted her with some gagging noises.

'They *are* a little nerdy, Cindy,' I said, as kindly as I could.

'Let's just do what we planned on doing,'

51

Pippa said. 'Write down four names each on separate pieces of paper, then jumble them all up and pick, say, eight, to be on the safe side.'

Fern tore a page out of her exercise book and we wrote the names down on little pieces of paper.

The eight names that won were: Paws, Mitten, Quasimodo, Paddle-steamer, King, Lafayette, Angel and Mozart.

'Who wrote Paddle-steamer!' Pippa said. 'You can't call a dog Paddle-steamer. Fern! Was that you?'

'No,' Fern said. 'Look at the writing. It was Cindy.'

Cindy shrugged. 'You said my original names were nerdy. I had to come up with some alternatives. That was all I could think of.'

Paddle-steamer? You know, there are times when I'd like to climb inside Cindy's head and check out what goes on in there. And she *seems* perfectly normal most of the time.

* * *

Amanda gave me my instructions at the end of school.

'The Eddie Eden CD is on the floor by my CD player,' she told me. 'All you've got to do is go straight home and pick it up. Then you go to the mall. You'll get there in plenty of time. But make sure you get to the front. Don't be polite, OK? Use your elbows a little.'

'Why didn't you bring the CD with you?' I asked. 'Then I could have gone straight to the mall.'

'Because I didn't think of it,' Amanda said. 'Have you got any more dumb questions, or can I go now?'

Cheryl Ruddick's head appeared around the corner of the hallway.

'Amanda!' she yelled. 'The bus is waiting for you!'

'Coming,' Amanda shouted. She gave me a last look. 'You won't let me down, Stacy?'

I grinned at her. 'No problem,' I said. 'I'll get you an autograph if it's the last thing I do.'

Amanda ran down the hall. 'You're a real pal, Stacy. I'll see you later this afternoon.'

I have to admit, I hadn't agreed to go to the mall just to please Amanda. I was kind of interested in seeing whether Eddie Eden looked the same in real life as he does on the TV and in all those photographs. I mean, can *anyone* look that glamorous in real life?

★ ★ ★

'Mom! I'm home,' I called, as I ran up the stairs to Amanda's room. I threw my school bag in through my door. There was a *mwrroop!* noise from my room as the bag landed.

'Benjamin!' I ran in. Benjamin was under the bed looking out at the bag. 'Oh, gee, I'm sorry, Benjamin,' I said, getting down on my hands and knees. 'Did I almost squish you.'

'Mrrp!' Benjamin came out from under the bed and rubbed up against me. Phew! Forgiven!

'I'm sorry. I don't have time to play,' I told him. 'I'm on an important errand for Amanda. You go back to sleep and I'll see you later.'

I ran into Amanda's room. What a mess! On one side was art-mess, and on the other was everyday-mess. And somewhere in between was Amanda's Eddie Eden CD.

'A-ha!' I found it and headed downstairs.

'Mom!' I called. 'I'm out again!'

'Where are you going, honey?' Mom called from the basement.

I ran to the door. 'To the mall for Amanda,' I yelled down at her.

'You be careful over there,' Mom called. 'It might get a little hectic. I don't want you brought home in a shoebox!'

'I'll be ultra-super-careful,' I called.

I was almost out the door when the phone rang.

I skidded to a halt and picked up the receiver.

'Hello?' I said.

'Stacy?'

'Yes.'

'Puppies!' Fern screamed down the phone. '*Puppies*! Hundreds and thousands of puppies. Millions of puppies! Puppies everywhere!'

'What? Already?'

I heard Fern take a deep breath. 'Mom says Hobo started this morning at around ten o'clock,' she gabbled. 'There are seven of them. You've never seen anything like it, Stacy! You've *got* to come over and see them.'

'I'll be there in ten minutes!' I said.

I was out of the house in seconds. I grabbed my bike and took off down the sidewalk like a rocket. I needed to see those pups, and I needed to see them *now*!

I cycled as fast as I could over to Fern's place. The front door was open.

Pippa, Cindy and Fern were sitting on the floor in the hallway, looking into the built-in closet.

'Shhh!' Pippa hissed as I went in.

I peered around the edge of the closet door.

Hobo was lying on her side in a big cardboard box lined with a blanket. And nuzzling and wriggling and climbing all over each other were her seven little puppies.

'Ohh!' I breathed. They were all wrinkly and wriggly and covered with the finest of fine fur. Their little ears were folded flat and their perfect little eyes closed. Every now and then one of them would make a little squeaky yelping noise as they clambered and crawled over each other. Two of them were white, two were brown and white, one was black and white and the other two were black and brown.

They climbed all over each other as they tried to get to Hobo's teats for a feed. Three of them were clamped on tight, and the others were squirming around, their little legs kicking and their noses burrowing blindly.

They were so funny and cute and perfect that you just wanted to gather them all up in your arms and hug them like crazy!

Fern giggled as the black-and-white puppy rolled on to its back and lay kicking its tiny little legs to try to get the right way around again.

Hobo looked real proud as her seven puppies clambered over her tummy. Every now and then one of them would get a lick and a nudge back toward the others.

'Here you go,' Fern's mom said, kneeling behind us and handing a bowl to Fern. 'See if Hobo would like this.'

'What is it?' asked Pippa. I noticed she still had the dog book with her. I guess she was planning on putting Hobo right, if and when she showed any signs of not being the perfect mother.

'It's egg and milk,' Fern's mom said. 'The protein will do her good.'

Fern reached into the box and put the saucer by Hobo's head. Wow! She sure was grateful for that! She finished the entire bowlful in about ten big laps.

'Oh, look!' Cindy squeaked.

One of the white puppies was doing a little mountaineering up Hobo's side.

'Can we touch them?' Cindy asked.

'I don't think that's a good idea today,' Fern's mom said. 'Let Hobo get used to them first. Just watch.'

And speaking of *watch*, I knew I had to watch the time. Puppies or no puppies, I had to be at the mall soon. But it was OK, my watch said three-thirty. There was plenty of time. All four of us knelt in the doorway of the closet, watching Hobo's little puppies feeding and falling over one another and kicking and nuzzling with their blunt little noses.

'I've made some lemonade, if anyone's interested,' Mrs Kipsak called from the kitchen. 'I think maybe it's time you left them in peace, girls. I expect Hobo would like some sleep now.'

'I guess so,' Fern said with a sigh. 'I could watch them all *day*!'

Cindy stretched as she got up off the floor.

'What time is it?' she asked.

I looked at my watch. It still showed three-thirty. 'It's five o'clock,' said Fern.

Arrgh! Five o'clock! My watch had stopped!

The mall! I should have been there over an hour ago.

At that very moment, I should have been kicking and struggling to get at Eddie Eden, instead of watching Hobo's puppies kicking and struggling to get at some of their mom's milk.

Amanda was going to kill me.

There was no doubt about that. Amanda was going to *kill* me.

Chapter Six

'I'll pick my bike up later!' I yelled as I ran down Fern's driveway.

Eddie Eden was supposed to be signing stuff until half-past five. That meant I still had a half-hour. I was pretty sure that wouldn't give me time to get there on my bike, but I should just make it if I went by bus.

I did some quick calculations as I hared along the road to the bus-stop. If the bus came within ten minutes, I'd be OK.

Ten minutes waiting for the bus.

Ten minutes to get to the Clearwater Mall.

Five minutes to get up to the third floor where Rocky's Record Store was.

Four minutes to pile-drive my way to the front of the store.

One minute to get Amanda's CD signed.

Perfect.

'Stacy!' I looked around as I heard the yell from behind me. It was Cindy, jumping up and down on the sidewalk and waving her arm in the air.

I waved back.

'You forgot *this*!' Cindy shouted. She was holding something in her hand. Something small and square and flat.

Amanda's CD!

I came to a screaming halt and ran back to meet her.

'Thanks,' I panted. 'I'll call you.'

I ran to the bus-stop. There were quite a few people already standing there. A good sign. The more people the better, because that meant there hadn't been a bus for a while.

Come on, bus! Come on, bus!

I stared down the road, willing a bus to appear. What was this – a bus-free zone all of a sudden? Had all the buses been scooped up by aliens? Is there some kind of blobby alien mother-ship up in the sky, come to Indiana on a field-survey of terrestrial public transport?

I looked at my watch. My rotten, crummy watch that had caused all my problems. I had got it started again by banging it against a wall. And it was still going. It showed nine minutes and fourteen seconds past five.

I looked again about two seconds later, and

it was nine minutes and fifty-five seconds past five!

How come time goes so quickly when you don't want it to? How come birthdays go by in a flash, but exam days drag on for ever? Oh, heck – I don't have time to worry about things like that.

Where's that bus?

Hooray! It came trundling up at exactly ten and a half minutes past five. That left me half a minute short on my calculations. I'd have to go like a rocket once it dropped me off at the mall.

Wonder-Stacy takes off into the air! *Whoosh* – out through the bus doors. *Zoom* – across the plaza. *Whee* – in through the revolving doors. *Yowlp* – out through the revolving doors again because someone gave them a shove and I didn't have time to get out inside the mall before I found myself out on the *outside* again.

Second time lucky, and I went streaking across the walkway, dodging and diving through the people.

'Oops, excuse me. Oh! Sorry.'

Why were there so many people in the way? I mean, don't they have any *homes* to go to?

I jumped on to the escalator and wormed my way up through the people.

Time check. Five twenty-two and forty seconds.

Bump! I crashed straight into a fat lady. It was like jumping into a mattress. *Boi-oing*! She didn't even *rock* as I picked myself up and zipped across to the escalator for the third floor.

Rocky's Record Store was along the main walkway and round to the left.

Time check. Five twenty-four and sixteen seconds.

I went racing around the corner and came to a stop. The whole width of the walkway was filled with people. You couldn't call it a queue. No one was *queueing*. Everyone was shoving and pushing, and some Eddie Eden song was blaring out over the noise.

I guess the crowd was mostly girls, but I could see a few older people and a few boys squished in amongst them. I could see the entrance to Rocky's Record Store above the crowd. There were window displays on either side. Posters of Eddie Eden and a big placard that read: *Here Today! The Fabulous Eddie Eden*!

Yeah, right. The fabulous Eddie Eden. And if I had a bulldozer, I might stand some chance of getting within ten feet of him.

Oh, well, I thought, *here goes nothing*. I took

a firm hold of Amanda's CD and dived into the crowd.

Sometimes being small and skinny has its up-side. I squirmed and wormed and wriggled and squiggled my way through the crowd.

Amanda would have been proud of me. It wasn't until the crowd got really tight-packed in the doorway that I was stopped from squeezing my way forward. And to think, this was *me* doing this. Stacy, who usually waits politely in line. Stacy, who always waits her turn. Grarrr! Stacy the Unstoppable! See how she flings the people out of her path! Witness the merciless way she tramples lesser mortals underfoot. *Arrgh*! Spot the way she gets squished in the doorway like a tube of toothpaste.

I was actually in the shop now. The music was really loud and I couldn't move a muscle as I was sort of carried along in the tide. Through the gaps in the mash of people I could see that barriers had been set up and that there were men in security-guard-type uniforms holding the barriers steady as we were shoved forward.

Eek! My feet left the ground. I hardly dared to breath out in case there wasn't room to breathe back in again. And I couldn't even see anything, apart from the back of a very wide girl directly ahead of me, into whose spine my nose was being shoved.

Suddenly the music cut out and a voice came over the public address system: 'Eddie Eden is no longer in the store,' it announced. 'Please remain calm and back away. Eddie Eden is no longer in the store.'

A big wail of disappointment went up from everyone, and there was a sudden surge from the back that squashed us even more tightly together and sent us skidding this way and that.

And then one of the barriers gave way and we all went spilling across the store.

That was it! I was done for! I dived for safety behind one of the security guards.

'Eddie Eden is no longer in the store,' repeated the voice over the public address system. It was sounding a little more panicky now. 'Please don't push. Hey! You people at the back! Don't push. Eddie's *gone*! He went out the back way. He's heading for his limo. Believe me! He's out of here!'

The message finally seemed to sink in and the pushing and shoving to get *into* the store turned into a pushing and shoving to get *out* again.

I peered around the back of the security guard.

'Wow!' he said, straightening his tie. 'Give me riot control any day.' I could see his point. It did kind of look like a tornado had just blown through the store.

A half-hearted message came over the public address system: 'There's plenty of Eddie Eden merchandise for sale at Rocky's Record Store,' it said. 'Step right up to the counter and ask for your copy of Eddie Eden's latest chartbuster. Get your Eddie Eden T-shirts. Eddie Eden buttons. Eddie Eden posters.' The voice let out a sigh of relief. 'Eddie Eden bandages?' it said. 'Eddie Eden neck-braces? *Whee-ooh*! Thank you and goodnight, Four Corners!'

I looked over towards the counter. Three assistants were standing there looking really relieved that the whole thing was over. There were flyers scattered all over the floor, advertising Eddie Eden's 'This Way to Paradise' tour.

Well, the security people might be relieved. Rocky the storekeeper and his worn-out assistants might be relieved. But that was because *they* didn't have an Eddie Eden-mad sister over on the other side of town, who was desperate to have her CD autographed.

I went over to the counter. 'Has he really gone?' I asked.

'I'm afraid so,' said one of the assistants.

I held up Amanda's CD. 'I wanted to get this signed,' I said. 'My sister's going to kill me.'

'Why don't you buy your sister an Eddie Eden T-shirt?' suggested the assistant. He held up a T-shirt with a photo of Eddie Eden on a surfboard and words made up of water splashes which said *Eddie Eden. This Way to Paradise*!

'Authorized merchandise,' said the assistant with a big smile. 'Only thirty-five dollars.'

'I can't afford *that*,' I said. 'Anyway – I need an autograph. That's what I came here for. Don't you have anything with Eddie Eden's autograph on it?'

They didn't.

I walked out of the store and headed for the escalator.

'*Hey, Amanda. Do you want the good news or the bad news first? The good news is that Fern's new dog has had seven gorgeous little puppies. The bad news? Uh, Eddie Eden got stomach cramps from eating too many English muffins and didn't make it to the signing.'*

No, no, that was no good. There was bound to be something on the local news about the signing. I wouldn't get away for long if I pretended to Amanda it hadn't happened.

'Hi, Amanda – hey, you're just going to laugh your head off when I tell you what happened –'

No, I don't think so. Laugh her head off? Knock *my* head *off*, more like.

'Hey, Amanda, I'm calling from the casualty department of the hospital. I tried my best, but I just got trampled underfoot. Yeah, don't worry. A few cracked ribs and a broken leg. I don't care about my injuries – I'm just sick that I didn't get Eddie's autograph for you.'

Hmm. Possible. But what would happen when I got home without any injuries? I could guess what would happen. I'd be sent straight back to the hospital for real.

'Dear Amanda, I am writing this to you from an airplane heading for China. You're probably wondering what happened to that autograph I promised you . . . '

And then it hit me.

Ka-powee! like a bolt out of the blue. I had the answer.

It was so simple.

All I needed was one thing. A copy of Eddie Eden's signature.

And then I needed one other thing. A pen. OK, so I needed *two* things.

And then all I needed was a few minutes of peace and quiet to practise Eddie Eden's signature a few dozen times.

Well? Why not? I mean, Amanda wouldn't know any different. And it's not like I'd really be cheating her or anything. It's not like she *paid* me to get Eddie Eden's signature. It's not like any *money* changed hands.

I agreed to do her a favour. And I'd have done it if Hobo hadn't chosen that day to have her puppies. I mean, come on, no one could blame me for temporarily forgetting about Eddie Eden's autograph when there are seven adorable puppies and one proud mom to look at.

I just hoped there wasn't a law against forging a pop star's signature for your sister.

Chapter Seven

OK. Question one. Where would I be most likely to find a copy of Eddie Eden's signature?

Amanda's room, that's where! Amanda was in the Eddie Eden Fan Club (big surprise, huh?). The thing was that, being a fan club member (Amanda was fan club member 57438/AA), Amanda received the following:

A bi-monthly newsletter,

An exclusive fan-club-only Eddie Eden button,

An Eddie Eden car-sticker,

Special fan-club-members-only offers on Eddie Eden merchandise.

And a *signed* photo of you-know-who. Except that you could tell that it wasn't a *real* signature – it was just a print of his signature.

But that didn't matter. The point was that it was a copy of Eddie Eden's signature. It was something I could use for my planned piece of forgery.

All I had to do now was get home before Amanda.

I didn't have a whole lot of time. A half hour, maybe.

This time the bus was on my side. It came along straight away and I was home in fifteen minutes.

Mom and Sam were in the living room. Sam was lying on his back on the rug, kicking and chortling. Mom was kneeling over him on all fours, ducking her head and making *rsssp!* noises with her mouth on his bare tummy.

'Is Amanda home?' I asked.

'Is your big sister home, sweetheart?' Mom cooed at Sam. 'Is she? *Rssp!* Is she home? Is Amanda home? *Rssp!* Who's got a big fat tum-tum! *Rsssp!*'

I couldn't help laughing. Mom is just so soppy when she gets like that with Sam.

'Mom!'

Mom shook her head and Sam grabbed at her hair.

'She's not home, is she? No, no, no, no, no. Amanda's not home.' Mom picked Sam up and rolled on to her back, holding him up in the air over her head. He was chuckling and wriggling and looking cuter than a newborn puppy. I really wanted to join in with the games, but I had to get that signature, or the only game I'd be playing would be Count the Bruises.

'Say, hi, Stacy,' Mom said to Sam.

'Eggo geggy!' Sam said.

Mom sat up with Sam in her lap. 'Did you hear that, Stacy? He said 'Hello, Stacy.'

Now. Sam can say a few things. You can't always figure out what he's trying to tell you, but you can generally make a good guess. Like 'Bik!' means 'I'd like a toy to play with', and 'Nummus' means, 'Yummy, this sure tastes good'. But I figured it was going to be some time before Sam was going to get around to saying 'Hello, Stacy.' I mean, babies just don't say words like *Stacy*.

But I knew why Mom was trying to make out that Sam could say 'Stacy'. It was because he could already say Amanda. Amanda is a much easier word for a baby to say. Sam actually says 'Anda', but it's pretty obvious what he means, because he only says it when Amanda's playing with him.

So, Sam can say 'Mama', 'Dadda' and 'Anda'. He even knows his own name: *Dam*. The ways things are going, Sam will be able to say 'Benjamin' before he can say 'Stacy'. It's not Sam's fault that I've got a difficult name, but it is kind of typical that I should have the one name in the whole house that he can't say! Still, I guess I could always change my name to 'Nummus'.

I went up to Amanda's room to set Step One of the Great Forgery Scam into motion.

The "signed" photo of Eddie Eden had place of honour over Amanda's bed. I knelt on her bed and looked at it. Eddie Eden smiled back at me with his deep suntan and his perfect teeth.

Oh no! My hand has gone out of control! My whole arm has been taken over by some alien force. It's willing me to take a pen and black out Eddie Eden's front teeth. I must resist!

Phew! That was *close*! I very nearly lost control, there.

The photo was signed, *To All My Fans, Eddie Eden*, across his left shoulder.

I got some paper from Amanda's desk and tried to copy the signature. The capital Es were like backward 3s, and the double D was like four circles – a little one and then a big one on top, and then another little one and a big one on top, followed by a squiggly line with a ring over the bit where the I was meant to be. I did my best to copy it, but I made the lines all wobbly and shaky. I looked at my attempt. Not good.

I could imagine Amanda's reaction. '*Excuse me, Stacy – what is* this?'

'*You're not going to believe this, Amanda, but just as Eddie was signing your CD, there was an* earthquake.'

My forgery wasn't even close. What I really needed to do was to take the photo away with me and spend some time getting it right. The problem being that Amanda would be certain to notice the Eddie Eden-shaped hole in her photo collection, and was pretty likely to jump to conclusions and figure out I'd taken it.

And then I had a brainwave. Tracing-paper! I could trace the signature and practise with *that*!

Amanda had to have some tracing-paper somewhere. I mean, she's got *everything* in her room, somewhere. It was just a case of finding it – and keeping an eye on the clock. I didn't want to meet up with Amanda before I'd managed to get a signature on her CD.

I found a roll of tracing-paper and carefully copied Eddie Eden's signature: still a little wobbly in places, but good enough to use as a guide.

I went into my own room and cleared a

space on my desk. I'd just got everything set, and was about to start forging, when I heard the front door open and Amanda's yell.

'I'm home! Stacy! I'm home!'

There was a galloping of feet up the stairs. I only just had time to dive under my desk and pull the chair up in front of me as a shield before Amanda came bursting into my room.

'Stacy! Did you get it? Stacy?'

I sent out my most powerful thought-waves: *Don't look under the desk. There is no one hiding under the desk. Stacy is not here. Turn around and leave the room.*

'Oh, heck!' Amanda said, turning around and walking out.

There are times when it's real useful to have the power to project thought-waves at people. Of course, that was the first time that it had ever *worked*.

I waited until I heard Amanda go back downstairs. Then I grabbed the tracing-paper and crept out of my room. The operation was going to take expert timing.

I heard Amanda talking to Mom in the living room.

'She's upstairs,' Mom said. Thanks Mom!

I tiptoed down the stairs and zipped around into the kitchen. Five seconds and I was out the back door. Fifteen seconds and I was around the front of the house and running at full speed down the street with the tracing-paper in one hand and Amanda's CD in the other.

I didn't run *all* the way to Cindy's house, but I did run *most* of the way. Which is why it took me three or four minutes to catch my breath and explain to Cindy what had happened. And it didn't help that Cindy was more interested in yakking about the puppies than about my problems with Eddie Eden's signature.

'We decided to drop Paddle-steamer as a name,' she told me. 'The two white puppies are going to be Angel and Paws.'

'I've got to try and copy Eddie Eden's signature,' I butted in. 'Hello? Cindy? Are you receiving me? Stacy calling Cindy. Is anyone ho-ome?'

'And the black-and-white one is going to be King,' Cindy said. 'What was that about Eddie Eden's signature? Oh, Stacy – you should have seen the one with the brown markings on its face. It's already started fighting with the others. Fern says we should call that one Quasimodo, because it's kind of strange-looking.'

'That's really fascinating, Cindy,' I said.

'But I've got to copy Eddie Eden's signature on Amanda's CD – and I've got to do it now.'

'Didn't you get to the mall in time?' Cindy asked, finally cottoning on to what I was talking about.

I took a deep breath and told her the whole story again.

'Let me see that signature,' Cindy said. I showed her the tracing-paper.

'Hmm,' she said, 'it's kind of wobbly.'

'That's because I was copying it from a picture pinned to Amanda's bedroom wall,' I explained.

'Let's go and give it a try,' Cindy said.

We went up to her room and she got out some paper.

I sat at her desk first and tried a copy.

Cindy looked at it over my shoulder. 'It's not very good,' she said. She was right. It wasn't. I tried again. And again. And again. I filled an entire sheet with feeble attempts at Eddie Eden's signature. I filled two sheets.

'You're doing it too slowly,' Cindy said. 'You've got to go, kind of – *squiggle* – really fast, otherwise it's always going to look shaky. Try to relax.'

I relaxed so much that I almost slid off the chair. OK. This was it. *Squiggle*.

'Hey,' Cindy said. 'That's not bad.'

I squiggled again. *Eddie Eden*. Squiggle. Eddie Eden. Eddie Eden. Eddie Eden.

'I've got it!' I said. 'Quick, hand me the CD while I'm hot.'

Cindy slid the booklet out of the front of the CD while I did a couple more practice runs.

'OK. Now!' I said. Cindy put the booklet in front of me and I did my perfected Eddie Eden squiggle over the picture of Eddie Eden walking on the beach.

'Well?' I said, not daring to look.

'It's great,' Cindy said. 'It'd fool me.'

I opened my eyes. It was a pretty good forgery, although I said it myself. It would have fooled me, too. The big question was – would it fool Amanda?

* * *

'Where the heck have you *been*!' Amanda yelled as I opened the front door. She was sitting on the stairs like a vulture waiting for its victim to let out its last gasp.

'I went to see Cindy,' I said, perfectly truthfully.

'Didyougetit? Whereisit? Gimmeit!'

'OK, OK,' I said. 'Calm down. It's here.'

Amanda pounced on the CD. '*Wahhh-eee-hahhh!*' she howled, dancing around in front of me like an Apache in a drought. 'You've got to tell me all about it. What does he look like up close? What was he wearing? Did he *say* anything.'

'He looked just like his photos,' I said. 'He was wearing the same stuff as on TV this morning, and he didn't say anything.'

'Oh, *you*!' Amanda exclaimed. 'You're hopeless!' She finished dancing around and looked at the signature a little too carefully for my liking.

'He did it in a big rush,' I said. 'There were hundreds of people there wanting autographs.'

Amanda stared at the autograph and then at me. Icy fingers crept up my spine.

'Oh, Stacy!' Amanda said, shaking her head.

'What?' Gulp. Had she somehow figured it out *already*?

'You could have asked him to put "To Amanda, with love",' Amanda said.

'Oh, right!' I said. 'I *do* beg your pardon, Amanda. I mean, I only got crushed half to *death* trying to get that for you. I'm really sorry I didn't ask him to write the Gettysburg Address on it while I was there.'

Amanda gave me a hug. 'I'm sorry,' she said. 'I didn't mean to complain. It's really great, Stacy.' She went running into the living room. 'Mom! I've got Eddie Eden's autograph!'

That's right, Amanda – you just keep believing that, and everything will be fine.

I guess you could say I had deceived her – but it was in a good cause, so what harm could it do? I was in Amanda's good books for once. She was cruising about with her feet thirty yards off the ground, and everything was right with the world.

Or it *would* have been, if it wasn't for Amanda's mega-Bimbo friend, Cheryl Ruddick.

Chapter Eight

Ah! Cheryl Ruddick? How can I *describe* you?
There are times when the word 'Bimbo' is so
inadequate. Saying that Cheryl Ruddick is a
Bimbo is a little like saying the house where I
live is made out of bricks. I mean, it *is* – but
there's so much more to it.

She isn't the most stupid of the Bimbo Brigade. (We call Amanda's friends the Bimbo
Brigade because they call *us* the Nerds.)
Rachel Goldstein is the dumbest of the
Bimbos.

And Cheryl isn't the vainest of them. Natalie Smith is the vanity queen of Four Corners,
with her long ash-blonde hair and her giggly
little-girlie voice.

But Cheryl is definitely my least favourite
Bimbo. She's got this hairstyle that looks like
she's stuck her tongue in an electric socket.
Or sometimes I think it makes her look more
like an angry porcupine. And the funny thing

is that she has it like that on *purpose*. She thinks it looks great.

You know when you're making horrible faces and your mom says, 'If the wind changes you'll get *stuck* like that?' Well, I guess that's what must have happened to Cheryl.

Someone must have said to her, 'Hey, Cheryl, make a face like a hyena!' And she did. And the wind changed. And now she has to go around all the time looking like a hyena. Which wouldn't be so bad, I guess, if not for the fact that she's got a laugh like a hyena, too.

Amanda and I were sitting on the wall outside school the following morning. It made a nice change for us to sit together like that, even though we were having two completely different conversations.

'It says here that Eddie Eden's favourite colour is blue,' Amanda said, reading from a magazine. 'That's amazing! *My* favourite colour is blue!'

'So we decided to call the black-and-white puppy King,' I told her. 'And the two black-and-brown ones are going to be called Mozart and Quasimodo. I bet you don't know who Quasimodo was.'

'He's just ended his two-year relationship

with supermodel Coral Holender,' Amanda read.

'What? Quasimodo?' I said.

'Eddie Eden!' Amanda exclaimed. 'I wish you'd pay attention when I'm talking to you.' She went back to her magazine. 'Eddie says, "It's very difficult to keep your personal life together when you're always on the road. I don't blame Coral for wanting something more. We're still friends." ' Amanda sighed.

'The white puppies are Paws and Angel,' I said.

' "Coral Holender says it's very difficult for two professional people who are always in the public eye to keep any kind of relationship together," ' Amanda read. 'Phooey!' she said. 'She just didn't *try* hard enough!'

Amanda's eyes went glassy as she gazed into the distance. 'I can see it now,' she sighed. 'I'll have my studio in our big house overlooking the beach in California. I'll have the whole of the top floor. There'll be canvases stacked everywhere, waiting to be shipped out to galleries of the world. And Eddie will have his own recording studio in the basement. And we'll fix it so that when he goes on tour with his band, I'll be holding exhibitions in . . . in . . . Paris and Rome and . . . and . . . that wet place. You know – the place with rivers instead of streets.' She looked at me. 'You know the place I'm talking about. The town with the gondoliers.'

'Detroit?' I said.

'No! Vienna!'

'You mean Venice,' I said. 'Venice, Italy.'

'Yeah, that's the one,' Amanda said. 'Anyway, like I was saying, if two people really wanted to be together, they wouldn't let their careers get in the way. I could be a world-renowned painter without feeling jealous of Eddie's career.'

'That's good of you,' I said. 'I just hope he can cope with how famous you're going to be.'

'Of course he will,' Amanda said. 'I could paint his album covers for him.' Her eyes suddenly went circular. 'Hey – I could send him one of those drawings I've done of him. I could send him a letter via his record company – and I could put one of my drawings of him in with it.' I could tell by the expression on Amanda's face that she'd gone into orbit with her fantasies.

'And then he'll write back,' Amanda said. 'And he'll ask me to do his next album cover. And we'll meet up, and he'll fall for me . . . and . . .'

'Hold up!' I said. 'Wait! Just a minute. Excuse me!'

Amanda stared at me. 'What?'

'Aren't you missing something here?' I said. 'Like, you're thirteen and he's twenty-six? That's a thirteen-year gap.'

'Yeah – but only temporarily,' Amanda said.

'Huh?'

'It might seem like a big gap *now*,' Amanda explained. But by the time Eddie is, say, thirty-five, I'll already be twenty-four – '

'Twenty-*what*?'

Amanda frowned. 'OK, twenty-two. But do you see what I mean? The older you get, the less the age difference matters.' She shook her head, giving me this real pitying look. 'You just don't understand this stuff.'

'Sure I do,' I said, patting her arm. 'You're going to be an artist, and you're going to live with Eddie Eden in a big beach house in California. I just hope you'll remember your folks back home when you're rich and famous.'

'I sure will,' Amanda said. 'I'll buy a retirement home for Mom and Dad in Miami.'

'And me and Sam?' I asked.

Amanda thought for a moment. 'Sam could become a record producer and help out with

84

Eddie's records.' She grinned. 'And you could be my maid.'

Before I could think of a good reply to that, we were interrupted by a loud bray of hyena laughter.

> *Multiple-choice question*
> *You are sitting on the wall outside Four Corners Middle School when you hear a noise that sounds like a laughing hyena. Is it:*
>
> A)   *A laughing hyena*
> B)   *Cheryl Ruddick?*

'Hi, Amanda,' Cheryl said as she came up to us with Natalie Smith and Rachel Goldstein in tow. 'All on your own? What are you reading?' she gave me a brief glance. 'Oh. Hi, Stacy.'

Did you spot that? "Hi, Amanda. All on your own? Oh. Hi, Stacy." *That's* why Cheryl is my least favourite of Amanda's friends. In Cheryl Ruddick's opinion, being with me is the same as being on your own. *Grr*! I wish Hobo's puppies were grown up. I'd sic 'em on her!

'There's an article about Eddie Eden,' Amanda said.

'You can keep him,' said Natalie, with a toss of her long blonde hair. 'I prefer Cal Hooper.'

'Yeah,' Rachel said. 'Cal Hooper's the *best*.' Rachel looks like a monkey, with these long skinny arms and legs and all this wiry carrot-coloured hair. Except that no monkey was ever as dumb as Rachel Goldstein.

'If Cal Hooper was twice as attractive as he is, he'd still only be half as good-looking as Eddie Eden,' Cheryl said.

'Yeah! Right!' Rachel said, looking a little confused.

'Eddie Eden's just some two-bit actor who couldn't carry a tune in a bucket!' Natalie said.

'Oh, yeah?' Amanda said. 'So how come Eddie Eden's record is at number two in the charts and Cal Hooper can't even get *arrested* since he split with his group?' (Cal Hooper was the lead singer with a group called Walking on Air. I'm not telling you that for any particular reason. I just thought you might like to know.)

'That's true,' Rachel said. 'Cal's really gone downhill since he went solo.'

'Whose side are you on?' Natalie asked her. 'I thought you just said you preferred Cal Hooper?'

'I do,' Rachel said. 'But that doesn't mean I don't prefer Eddie Eden as well.'

'You can't prefer Eddie Eden to Cal Hooper, and prefer Cal Hooper to Eddie Eden at the same time!' Natalie yelled.

'I can, too,' Rachel said. 'Sometimes I like Cal Hooper's songs better, and sometimes I like Eddie Eden's songs better. What's wrong with that?'

Natalie gave Rachel a very expressive look. I was sitting there trying not to laugh. There are times when listening to Rachel Goldstein is better than watching a comedy show on TV.

'Well, it's a good thing you don't prefer Eddie Eden,' Cheryl said. 'Or you'd just *die* of jealousy when you saw *these*.'

She pulled out a small envelope from the inside pocket of her jacket. She opened it really slow, like they open the envelope containing the winner's name at those award ceremonies.

Cheryl pulled two tickets out of the envelope.

Amanda gave a gasp and snatched them out of Cheryl's hand. 'Wheedoogedeese?' she screamed. (Amanda tends to get a little incoherent when she gets excited. I think she was *trying* to say, 'Where'd you get these?')

I leaned over Amanda's arm.

Eddie Eden. This Way to Paradise. Fairfield Hall. Four Corners.

They were two tickets for Eddie Eden's concert that Saturday night.

'Howdoogeddem?' Amanda wailed. 'Imeen – whawhewhoo – '

'Pretty impressive, huh?' Cheryl said, plucking the tickets back out of Amanda's hand and waving them under Natalie's nose.

'It's a pity you don't like Eddie Eden,' she said. 'Because one of these tickets is going spare.'

Amanda looked like one of those cartoons where the top of some character's head is about to blow off. 'How'd you get them?' she finally managed to ask. 'Cheryl! I thought you said your folks wouldn't let you *go*!'

'I can deal with my folks,' Cheryl said.

Rachel was staring at the tickets with her mouth hanging open. 'But your mom said there was no way she'd let you go,' Rachel said. 'Even after you'd threatened to go on hunger strike and lock yourself in your room for a week.'

'I did no such thing,' Cheryl said.

'You did, too,' Rachel said. 'I was there!'

'So she changed her mind,' Cheryl snapped,

glaring at Rachel. 'My mom can be reasonable.'

'She *can*?' Amanda said. 'Since when?'

Cheryl's face split into a big grin. 'Since she doesn't know anything about it.'

'You mean you bought them without asking?' Natalie asked. 'Wow – are you going to be in trouble when she finds out!'

'Who says she's going to find out?' Cheryl said. 'I've got a plan that means she won't know a thing about it.'

'What kind of plan?' Amanda asked, her eyes glued to the two tickets in Cheryl's hand.

Cheryl grinned. 'I was kind of hoping you'd ask me that,' Cheryl said. 'Because you, Amanda Allen, Eddie Eden fan and best friend of mine, are the very person who's going to make sure my brilliant plan comes off. If you fancy going to the concert, that is.'

Uh-oh! I didn't like the sound of that. And I liked it even less when Amanda said, 'I'll do it! Whatever it is! I'll *do it*!'

Chapter Nine

'I've had some brilliant ideas in my time,' Cheryl said. 'But this one is the *greatest*.'

'Yeah? Yeah?' Amanda urged her. 'Tell me!' But Cheryl was enjoying the spotlight too much just to come right out with her 'brilliant' plan.

'So what are you going to do, Cheryl?' Natalie asked in a real sarcastic voice. 'Put sleeping pills in your mom's coffee? That's the only way you're going to get out of the house on Saturday night.'

'Not if I'm spending the night with a friend,' Cheryl said. 'Not if there's a slumber party . . .' she looked meaningfully at Amanda, '. . . at a *friend*'s house on Saturday night.'

'Hey, a slumber party!' Rachel said. 'Great! We haven't had one in months.'

'Rachel?' Cheryl said.

'Yeah?'

'Shut up.' She looked at Amanda. 'Do you

see what I mean? I tell my mom that I'm staying over at your place. And then we can sneak out to the Fairfield Hall . . .' Her voice rose as she came to the climax of her brilliant plan, '. . . *and* we can see Eddie Eden!'

Amanda and Cheryl danced around on the sidewalk, hugging each other.

'Are you up for it?' Cheryl yelled.

'Do fish swim?' Amanda shrieked. 'Does Eddie Eden make great records? Yeah – sure, I'm up for it!'

'Excuse me,' Natalie said, her voice as cold as ice, 'but where is Amanda supposed to say she's sleeping?'

Cheryl laughed. 'At my house!' she said. 'Don't you get it yet, bean-brain?' She stopped jigging around with Amanda. 'Watch my lips very carefully, Natalie. I tell my mom I'm staying over at Amanda's house. Amanda tells her mom that she's staying over with me.' Cheryl pointed to herself and then to Amanda. 'And then the two of us – that's Amanda and me, OK? – the two of us take *these* tickets to the Fairfield Hall to see Eddie Eden in concert.'

'*Wo-o-o-ow*,' Rachel breathed. 'That's so cool!'

There was a smug kind of smile on Natalie's

face. 'And what do you do *after* the concert?' she asked Cheryl.

Cheryl frowned at her. 'What do you mean, "What do you do after the concert?" We come home, dummy. What do you expect us to do?'

'Whose home?' Natalie asked.

Cheryl opened her mouth to reply, but stopped dead. She stood there with her mouth hanging open and a blank look on her face. It looked to me as though Natalie had put her finger on the one big flaw in Cheryl's "brilliant" plan. If Cheryl was supposed to be sleeping at our house, and Amanda was supposed to be sleeping at Cheryl's house, where the heck were the two of them actually going to spend the night?

Amanda groaned.

I jumped down off the wall. 'Nice try, Cheryl,' I said. 'That plan was very nearly *average.*'

'Get lost, Nerd,' Cheryl said.

I caught sight of Fern and Pippa over on the other side of the teachers' car park.

'Have fun with your tickets,' I said to Cheryl. 'Maybe you can raffle them?'

I ran over to Fern and Pippa before Cheryl could come up with a reply.

The last thing I heard from them was Rachel saying, 'What about this slumber party, then?'

I knew how much Amanda wanted to see Eddie Eden's concert, but I was kind of glad that it looked like Cheryl's plan wasn't going to work. It all sounded a little risky to me – even without the problem of where they were going to sleep.

'How are the puppies?' I asked Fern. 'Have their eyes opened yet?'

'Of course they haven't,' Pippa said, rummaging in her bag. She pulled out her dog book and flipped through it. ' "Puppies' eyes will not open for ten to fourteen days",' she read.

'Poor little things,' I said. 'Fancy not being able to see your mommy. What if one of them wanders off in the wrong direction and gets lost?'

'They squeak,' Fern said. 'Quasimodo went crawling off and got tangled up in the blanket. He squeaked like crazy until Hobo pulled him back.'

Pippa started going through her bag again. 'I've got the photocopies of the poster,' she said. She pulled out a roll of paper and unwound it.

The four of us had designed a poster and

Pippa's mom had agreed to photocopy it for us. It had *DOG FOUND* in big letters at the top. Underneath we'd carefully printed a description of Hobo – including the fact that she was expecting puppies. At the bottom was Fern's address and phone number.

'So where do we put them?' Fern asked.

'In local shops,' Pippa said. 'And in the library. And we can pin some to trees in the streets near where you live. Someone's bound to recognize the description.'

'And what if no one does?' Fern said.

'Then I guess that means Hobo is a stray,' Pippa said.

'Which also means we've got seven puppies to find homes for,' I said. 'How long before they can leave their mom?'

Pippa consulted the book again. 'It says here that pups should be weaned at about six weeks.' She looked up at us. 'I guess that means they can leave their mom about the same time.'

Cindy joined up with us a few minutes later and the four of us spent the time before home-room talking about the puppies and deciding where we were going to put up the posters.

Six weeks, huh? That would give me plenty of time to work on Dad about letting us have a puppy. Once I'd got Dad on my side, he'd be able to convince Mom. Which would only leave me with one obstacle.

Benjamin.

How was I going to convince Benjamin that a new puppy would be a real neat idea?

Oh, well – plenty of time to worry about that. I mean, dogs and cats sometimes get on well together. I read a book about it not so long ago. *The Incredible Journey*. All about two dogs and a cat who travel right across Canada together. *They* got along OK. So why shouldn't Benjamin get along with a brother or sister puppy dog?

I was still thinking about this at break. The four of us were sitting on a bench, watching some older kids playing basketball, when I was grabbed from behind and dragged right off the bench.

'What the heck!' It was Amanda.

'I need to talk to you,' she said, hauling me away while Cindy and the others sat staring over their shoulders at us.

'I think Amanda wants to talk to me.' I called to my pals as I was yanked around a corner. 'I won't be long!'

Amanda took me around the corner of the

building. She had a very strange look in her eyes.

Uh-oh! The forged autograph! I just *knew* what had happened. She'd shown it to someone, and they'd said '*That's not really Eddie Eden's signature.*' And Amanda will have said, '*Yes, it is.*' And they'd have said, '*No, it isn't. Eddie Eden was using a Magic Marker that day, not a ballpoint pen.*'

'I can explain!' I said.

Amanda stared at me. 'What?'

'I panicked,' I said. 'I didn't know what else to do. I knew you'd be – '

'Will you shut up and listen to me?' Amanda said. 'I don't know what you're talking about, but if you'll shut up for thirty seconds, I want to *talk* to you.'

'Oh.' She didn't sound mad. Maybe it was nothing to do with the autograph after all. 'OK.' I clamped my lips tight shut and waited for her to say whatever it was she wanted to say.

'You know I never really mean it when I call you names,' Amanda said. 'And you know I'd always help you out if you ever needed anything.'

'I guess,' I said.

'And I'm *sure* you'd always help me out if I

ever needed anything,' Amanda said. She gave me a hopeful look. '*Wouldn't* you?'

'I guess,' I said suspiciously.

'Right!' Amanda said. 'We'd both help each other out. That's what sisters do, right?'

'What do you want?' I asked.

'It's hardly *anything*,' Amanda said. 'I mean – really – it's *nothing*.'

'Fine,' I said. 'I can do *nothing* for you – no problem. Can I go now?'

'Well, maybe it's a little more than nothing,' Amanda said.

'Amanda, are you going to *tell* me what you want,' I asked, 'or do you want to leave it until after we graduate?'

'All I want you to do is to open a door for me at home,' Amanda said. 'It's as simple as that.'

I lifted my arm and gave her a little tap on the side of the head. 'I think your brain's come loose again,' I said. 'Let's see if I can kind of nudge it back into place.' *Tap!* 'Is that any better?'

Amanda frowned for a moment. Then she remembered she needed my help and she gave me one of her best cheerleader smiles.

'Cheryl and I have decided we're going to the concert on Saturday night,' she said. 'What we want you to do is to let us in afterwards without Mom or Dad hearing.'

'Let you in where?' I asked.

'Home, of course,' Amanda said.

'Oh, right. Our home?'

'That's it,' Amanda said. 'I'm going to tell Mom and Dad that I'm staying overnight with Cheryl. Then we're going to take a bus over to the concert. But afterwards, we're going to come back to our house to spend the night. But Mom and Dad mustn't know we're there, see? So you've got to let us in without them knowing.'

'And how do you explain how you got there on Sunday morning?' I asked. 'Teleportation?'

'We won't be there by the time Mom and Dad get up on Sunday,' Amanda said. 'We'll sneak out really early. All we need you to do is to keep your eyes open for us on Saturday night, and let us in the back way.'

I could see why it would be necessary for Amanda to get some inside help. Our front door is always double-locked last thing at night, which means you can't get it open from the outside even if you've got a key. And the back door is bolted from the inside when we go to bed.

98

'Are you sure this is such a brilliant idea?' I asked her. 'What if you get caught?'

'How can we possibly get caught?' Amanda said. 'Mom and Dad will think I'm with Cheryl; Cheryl's mom will think we're over here.' She put her arm around me. 'And only Cheryl, you and me will know the truth.'

'I don't know,' I said. 'Mom would go crazy if she found out.'

'She won't find out,' Amanda said. 'And what Mom doesn't know about won't hurt her.' She gave me a friendly squeeze – kind of like the sort of squeeze you'd get from a hungry boa constrictor. 'You'll help me out, won't you, Stacy?'

'Uh . . . I . . . I don't know if I want to get involved with this, Amanda,' I said.

A deadly smile fixed itself to the front of Amanda's face. 'I don't think you've quite understood, Stacy,' she said, her arm tightening around my shoulders. 'You wouldn't want to let me down over this, Stacy. You really *wouldn't*!'

'I wouldn't?'

Amanda shook her head. 'You definitely wouldn't.' I looked into Amanda's face. She had a look in her eyes that told me she'd make my life unbearable if I didn't go along with her.

'Oh, OK, then,' I said while I still had a little breath left in my body. 'I'll help you.'

Amanda let me go and gave a whoop!

'This way to paradise!' she yelled. 'Edd-EE! Edd-EE!'

She went prancing off, punching the air with her fists, and leaving me wondering exactly what I'd let myself in for.

Chapter Ten

'For the last time,' Amanda howled, 'there isn't a slumber party! There never *was* a slumber party!'

Rachel blinked at her.

'We're only *pretending* there's a slumber party so that my folks and Cheryl's mom will let us out on Saturday night.' Amanda spoke very slowly. 'So. We. Can. Go. To. The. Concert.'

'Ohhhh . . .' Rachel made this big, knowing grin. 'I get it!'

'Finally!' Amanda sighed.

It was after school. I'd been thinking about Amanda's idea all afternoon, and I'd decided that I really needed to have a chat with her about it. I mean, *someone* had to point out the problems that might come up – especially as that someone (me!) was likely to get in almost as much trouble with Mom and Dad as Amanda was. It's called being an *accomplice*.

I planned on going over to Fern's house a little later, but first of all I wanted to make it perfectly clear to my big, dumb sister that I wasn't going to have anything to do with her hare-brained scheme.

I waited until Rachel had wandered off.

'Amanda,' I said. 'I've been thinking about what we were talking about earlier.'

'How are the puppies?' Amanda asked.

'They're fine,' I said. 'But we really need to talk about this plan of yours, Amanda.'

'Have you given them names yet?' Amanda asked. I definitely got the impression she was trying to change the subject.

'Yes. I was telling you about it earlier, if you'd been listening. The thing is, Amanda – '

'Have you decided which one you'd like to keep,' Amanda interrupted. 'You know – after I've helped you persuade Mom to let you have one. You know, like I *promised* I would. I guess Fern will let you have the pick of the litter, huh?'

'I guess so,' I said.

'I've worked out how to convince Mom,' Amanda said. 'I'm going to tell her I'll take half the responsibility for looking after the puppy. We'll tell Mom she won't have to do a thing.'

'You would?' I said.

'Sure, I would,' Amanda said. 'We're sisters, right? And sisters *help each other out*, don't they? You've promised to help me on Saturday night, so it's only fair that I keep my promise to help you get one of Fern's puppies.' She smiled. 'If you choose a boy dog, we could call it Eddie. How's that sound?'

They've already got names,' I said. 'Amanda, are you really sure this is such a good idea?'

'I thought you desperately wanted a puppy,' Amanda said. 'Have you changed your mind?'

'I don't mean about the puppy,' I said. 'I meant about you and Cheryl going to the concert. You know what Mom thinks about it. What if you get caught?'

'You are such a baby, sometimes,' Amanda said. 'We're not going to get caught.'

It wasn't working. I had to come up with another angle.

'Are you sure those tickets are *real*?' I said. 'How do you know they're not forgeries?' (I guess I had the idea of forgeries on my mind right then. I can't imagine *why*!)

'They're real, all right,' Amanda said. 'Cheryl went over to the theatre and bought them from the ticket office.'

'Where did she get the money from?'

'She raided her vacation money,' Amanda said. 'Just like *I*'ll have to, in order to pay for the ticket I'm buying off her.'

'Oh, I thought she was giving you the ticket,' I said.

'Yeah, right,' Amanda said. 'They're not *cheap*, you know.' She smiled. 'But it'll be worth it! To see Eddie Eden in the flesh at last. To be under the same roof as him!'

'Oh, puh-lease!' I said. 'Excuse me while I get a bucket to be sick in!'

'You're too much of a kid to understand the passion that throbs in my heart!' Amanda said.

I stared at her. '*What* did you say?'

'It's from Eddie Eden's new single,' Amanda said, grabbing me by the wrists and dancing me around in circles as she sang:

'You'll never understa-ee-ay-ee-ay-and,
My heart's at your coma-ee-ay-ee-ay-
    and,
You'll never know-woh-woh,
The passion that throbs in my heart, for
    you-woo-woo,
The love that li-i-i-ies im my-y-y-y hea-
    a-a-art!'

'Whoo! Amanda,' I said, as I spun around. 'You never told me you couldn't sing!'

'I can sing better than you!' Amanda said, swinging me around even faster. 'Can't I? Admit it.'

'Wuurrgh,' I gurgled as the street whooshed around me. 'Amanda, quit it! I'm getting dizzy.'

We both started laughing as we came to a giddy stop.

Amanda put her arm around my shoulders, panting a little from the spin.

'I'll buy you a bag of potato chips on the way home,' she said. 'How's that?'

'Is that my reward for helping you out?' I said.

'A good deed is its own reward,' Amanda said.

'Says who?'

'I don't know,' Amanda said.

'I'll bet it was some real cheapskate,' I said. 'Anyway, I'm going to Fern's to see the puppies. Tell Mom I'll be home later.'

The puppies were just as gorgeous as ever. When I got to Fern's house, all the puppies but one were curled up in a heap in one corner of the box. The other one was padding about, rubbing itself along the side of the box as if it was trying to get out.

'That's so sweet,' Cindy said, carefully stroking the black-and-brown puppy with her finger. 'Look at its little face.'

Hobo lifted her head and watched Cindy as she stroked the side of her finger along the puppy's back.

'It's OK, Hobo,' Fern said, petting her head. 'We're not going to hurt your puppies.'

'That one's really adventurous,' Pippa said. 'I'll bet that one's going to be the cleverest.' She looked at Fern. 'Is it Mozart or Quasimodo?'

'It's Quasimodo,' Fern said. 'Mozart has got three black socks – Quasimodo only has two.'

I reached into the box and gave Quasimodo a gentle stroke. His fur felt like velvet against my finger. He sort of plopped on to his side and waggled his feet in the air.

'That's the one I'd have, if I could have a puppy,' Cindy said.

I looked at Quasimodo. He sure was cute. I so hoped that we'd be able to persuade Mom to let us have a puppy. I was sure that Benjamin wouldn't mind having a little brother, even if it *was* a dog.

I kept my fingers crossed as I walked home.

I even tried keeping my toes crossed, but I couldn't walk properly like that. So I crossed my arms instead, and, just for an extra piece of good luck, I crossed my eyes.

'Stacy?' Mrs Lloyd from next door asked as I walked past her in the street. 'Are you feeling OK?'

I uncrossed my arms and my eyes. 'I'm fine,' I said. 'I'm just wishing for a whole load of luck right now. Mega-huge amounts of luck.'

Mom and Amanda were in the living room as I walked in.

Sam was sitting on the floor with one of his toys. It was a yellow box with coloured shapes on it. When Sam bashed his fist down on a shape, an electronic voice would say, 'Yellow triangle' or 'Green square'. And it had a load of squares with pictures on. When he hit the one with an apple, it would say 'A is for apple'. Dad brought it back from one of his trips to Chicago. Mom said Sam was far too young to appreciate it, but Sam didn't seem to care. He just sat there bashing away at the box while it said 'H is for horse', or 'T is for tree'.

'Hi, everyone,' I said.

And then it happened. A little miracle. Sam looked up at me and said, 'Tacy!'

I just stared at him. 'Sam?'

He hammered his fists down on the box.

'Blue circle,' said the electronic voice.

'Tacy! Tacy!' Sam said.

'Sam, you can say my name!' I thumped down on to my knees and gave him the biggest hug.

'I taught him to say it,' Amanda said. 'Isn't that neat? He knows *all* our names now.'

Mom smiled. 'He sure is a clever little angel,' she said. 'He'll be walking before we know it. And the next thing we know, he'll be at school.'

Sam giggled and gurgled as I sat him in my lap and helped him to play with his speaking box.

'Oh, by the way,' Amanda said to Mom, 'Cheryl's invited me to stop the night with her on Saturday. Is that OK?'

'*This* Saturday?' Mom asked.

'Yeah. Why?' Amanda said. 'We aren't doing anything, are we?'

'Saturday?' Mom said. 'No, I don't think so. But you don't want to be up all night, Amanda. I know what you and Cheryl are like when you get together.'

'It's a Saturday night,' Amanda said. 'It's not like we've got to go to school the next day or anything.'

'All the same, I don't want you sitting up all night talking with Cheryl. You know what you're like when you miss your sleep. Perhaps it'd be better if Cheryl was to come over here. At least I can keep my eye on you, then. I'll be able to make sure you get to sleep at a reasonable time.

'Cheryl's mom can keep an eye on us,' Amanda said. 'What's the big problem?'

I had to admit, I couldn't figure out why Mom was making such a big deal out of this. It wasn't as if Amanda hadn't ever stayed over at a friend's house before. And Mom hadn't ever made a fuss about her staying up late when she had people over.

'There's no problem,' Mom said. 'I just don't want you staying up all night and then being too tired to do anything the next day.'

'The next day is Sunday,' Amanda said. 'What's to do on a Sunday?'

'You never know,' Mom said. 'Your father might like to take us all out for a drive or something.'

'Where to?' I asked. 'Where's Dad taking us?'

'I didn't say he *was* taking us anywhere,' Mom said. 'I just mentioned that he *might* want to take us out. That's all.' She gave

Amanda a peculiar smile. 'Of course you can spend the night at Cheryl's house. I'll just give Mrs Ruddick a call to make sure it's OK with her.'

'There's no need to do that,' Amanda almost shrieked.

'It's only polite,' Mom said. 'Mrs Ruddick always calls here when Cheryl sleeps over.'

'But I haven't even discussed it with Cheryl yet,' Amanda said. 'I only just had the idea.'

'Oh. You made it sound like it was already arranged,' Mom said. 'Didn't you say "Cheryl's invited me to stop the night"?'

'No,' Amanda said. 'I said I was going to see if Cheryl would like me to stay.'

'That's not what you said,' Mom said.

'Yes it was,' I said. 'Amanda said she was going to ask Cheryl to invite her to stay.'

Mom looked puzzled.

'G is for goose,' Sam's yellow box said, as he gave it a good whack with his foot. 'F is for flower'.

Mom shook her head. 'Well,' she said, 'you arrange it with Cheryl and then I'll give Mrs Ruddick a call.' She stood up. 'But right now I'd better get dinner started. Your father should be home soon.'

Sam squirmed and his elbow came down on the keyboard.

'P is for puppy,' said the box.

'Hey? Did you hear that?' I called after Mom. ' "P is for puppy"!'

'Cute,' Mom said as she walked down the hall to the kitchen. 'Even the toys are lined up against me!'

'Oh, heck!' Amanda breathed. 'Now what am I going to do? I can't let Mom call Cheryl's mother. And I forgot that Cheryl's mother always calls here when Cheryl stays!'

'That's the way it goes,' I said. 'I guess you won't be needing me to open any doors for you now.'

'Don't count on it,' Amanda said with a determined glint in her eyes. 'I'm not finished yet. I'm going to *get* to that concert on Saturday if it's the last thing I do!'

'N is for nut!' said the electronic box as Sam gave it another whack.

'It sure is,' I said, giving Amanda a hard look. I cuddled Sam. 'E is for Eddie Eden,' I told him. 'And C is for concert. And M is for mommy. And G is for grounded when Mom finds out that Amanda and Cheryl went to the concert without permission.'

I could have gone on:

A is for Amanda,
B is for Bimbo,
C is for Cheryl,
D is for disaster!
E is for grounded for ever!

Chapter Eleven

I was in my room, discussing the puppy situation with Benjamin.

'I know you don't get on too well with Whisky,' I said. 'But Quasimodo won't be anything like that.' Whisky was the terrier belonging to Mr and Mrs Lloyd from next door. Benjamin would sit on the garden fence and hiss at Whisky, and Whisky would jump up and down like a jack-in-the-box, yapping and growling at Benjamin.

Whisky must be a little dumb, because the one time he *did* manage to corner Benjamin, he got a real fierce swipe across the muzzle and went running in through the dog-flap with his tail between his legs.

Not that Benjamin always comes out on top. Whisky recently had Benjamin trapped up the tree at the bottom of the Lloyds' garden and it took three of us to get him down.

'You see,' I told Benjamin. 'Quasimodo will

just be a little puppy.' I cupped my hands together. 'No bigger than this. So you'll have to look after him.'

Benjamin was ignoring me. He was falling asleep on my legs. He'd been sitting up on my knees when I'd started talking to him about a new addition to the family.

(I started off with the same stuff that Mom said to us when she was expecting Sam. You know: happy event, bundle of joy, wonderful surprise and so on.)

After a few minutes, Benjamin started nodding off. He lay down along my legs with his chin on his paws.

By the time I'd got on to the part about all the fun they could have playing together, Benjamin was draped across my legs, fast asleep.

I had things to do – apart from being a cat-bed for the rest of the night. I tried sliding my legs out from under him without disturbing him. He gave me an irritated look and marched down to the bottom of the bed. *Thud*! He lay down with his back to me. A sure sign that he was annoyed with me.

'I'm sorry,' I said. 'But I've got to get to work on Dad.'

I'd decided that the best way to get Dad on

my side was to show him that I was taking the business of having a puppy very seriously.

Which is why I'd borrowed Pippa's dog book. The plan was that Dad would find me studying the dog book all the time. I wouldn't say things like. 'I'd really, *really* like a puppy.' I'd say stuff like, 'Did you know that puppies can be introduced to minced meat or chicken, or flaked fish and cereal by the time they're four weeks old?' That way Dad would know I was doing plenty of serious research and he could go away to Mom and help convince her that I was approaching the whole business in a thought-out and grown-up way.

I went downstairs, reading the dog book as I went, just in case Dad came out into the hall.

I stood outside the living-room door, going through the book for an interesting bit on puppies that I could read quietly to myself, sitting on the couch.

Well, you've got to be a little smart, and I figured that my *intelligent* approach had to be better than standing in front of the TV with an *I WANT A PUPPY AND I WANT IT NOW!* T-shirt on.

Mom and Dad were talking.

I didn't catch much of it, but what I *did* hear was kind of interesting.

'We agreed that it should be a surprise,' Dad was saying.

'Yes, I know,' Mom said. 'But it's very difficult. She's talking about it all the time. I very nearly came out and told her this afternoon. You don't know what it's like, trying to keep it a secret.'

'She doesn't suspect a thing,' Dad said. 'It'll be worth it to see the look on her face when we tell her.'

'I guess so,' Mom said. 'But it isn't *easy*.'

A thrill went right through me. It started in my tummy and went zooming up and down my arms and legs. Could it be? No, surely not. But what else? A surprise! And Mom had nearly told me this afternoon. It could only mean one thing! They'd decided I could have a puppy after all.

I ran into the living room. Mom and Dad were sitting on the couch. I jumped over the back with a yell of happiness and landed upside down between them with my legs waving in the air.

'Stacy!' Mom yelled. 'What on earth are you doing?'

'I'm happy,' I yelled, upside down. 'You're the best Mom and Dad in the entire world!'

Dad laughed. 'What made you suddenly decide that?' he asked, grabbing my legs and trying to tie them in knots while I wriggled and giggled.

'Nothing!' I yelled. 'I'm just really happy.'

Dad started tickling me.

Shriek! My dad is an expert tickler.

'Mind the furniture!' Mom yelled, as Dad chased me all round the floor. He caught me by the ankles and pulled me up so I was hanging upside down.

'Look what I've caught!' he said. 'The longest eel in the world!' I did some eel-wriggling while he carried me across to the couch and dumped me in Mom's lap.

'Oof!' Mom gasped as I landed on her. 'You're getting too big for this kind of thing.'

'Never!' Dad said. 'She's still my little girl!'

I sat up, pulling my clothes straight. I gave Mom a big hug and kissed her.

'Thanks, Mom,' I said. 'And I promise you won't have to do a *thing*! I'll do everything.'

She gave me a puzzled look. I put my hand over my mouth. Oops! I wasn't supposed to know yet. They'd wanted it to be a surprise.

'I didn't hear anything,' I said with a grin. 'Honest. I didn't hear a *word*!'

'Stacy – what are you talking about?' Mom asked.

I laughed. 'Nothing,' I sang. 'Nothing at all!'

I ran up to Amanda's room to tell her the good news.

'They're going to let me have a puppy,' I screeched. 'I just heard them talking about it. But they want it to be a surprise for me, so don't tell them I know, OK?'

'Typical,' Amanda said gloomily. 'Mommy's little favourite always gets what she wants.'

I'd been too excited with my news to notice how fed up she was looking.

'What's the problem?' I asked.

'Oh, nothing,' Amanda snapped. 'Only that I won't be able to go to the concert.'

'Why not?' I asked.

'Because, dummy, if I say I'm staying with Cheryl, Mom's going to call Cheryl's mother. And what's Cheryl's mother going to say? She's going to say, "That's strange, I thought Cheryl was staying with Amanda tonight."' Amanda looked miserably at me. 'I think they just might guess that we'd lied to them.'

'Oh, I see,' I said. 'Gee, I'm sorry, Amanda.'

'Not half as sorry as I am,' Amanda said.

'Hey, wait a minute,' I said, an idea was just coming to me. 'You were going to sneak in after the concert, OK? So why can't you sneak *out* before the concert. Sneak off to the concert and sneak back again. I can still let you in.'

'But I'd be gone all evening,' Amanda said. 'They'd notice I wasn't around. Unless you think I could fool them with a cardboard cut-out.' Her face suddenly lit up as though a light-bulb had been switched on in her head.

'Wait a minute,' she said, giving me a look that made alarm bells ring in my head. 'This might just work.' She got up from her slumped position on the bed. 'If you *covered* for me on Saturday evening, it's possible I'd get away with it.'

'Now, just hold on,' I said. 'I wasn't volunteering to help you. I'm just the brains of this organisation – I'm not taking the risks, thank you very much.'

'But there won't be any risk,' Amanda said, warming to the idea even more. 'I could say I wanted an early night after dinner on Saturday. Then I could pretend to go up to my room. But really I'd sneak out of the house and meet up with Cheryl.' She grinned. 'And then you could let me back in afterwards, just like you promised you would.'

'And what if Mom or Dad come up to your room?' I asked.

'I'll bunch up some pillows so it looks like I'm asleep.' Amanda said. 'I've seen it done in movies. It's easy.'

'What time will you have to leave for the concert?' I asked.

'About seven o'clock, I guess,' Amanda said.

'So what if they come up here at half-past seven?' I said. 'They're going to think it's pretty weird that you've gone to bed that early. You'll have to think of a way of keeping them out of your room.'

'Like how?' Amanda groaned.

'How should I know?' I said. 'This is your whacky plan. I don't want anything to do with it.'

Amanda smiled at me. 'But you're so smart, Stacy,' she said. 'You're really good at this kind of thing. I was only saying to Cheryl the other day, "Stacy is one of the smartest people I know." '

'You were?'

'Sure, I was. I'm always defending you, Stacy. You know that.'

Hmm. Get out the sleds and salt the roads. Snow-job alert!

'If you want a reason why you could be up here all evening,' I said, 'why not tell Mom and Dad that you're going to be working on a painting, and that you don't want to be disturbed.'

'Yes! That's it!' Amanda said. 'It's perfect!'

'It's crazy,' I said. 'And if it all goes wrong, I'm going to tell Mom and Dad that I didn't know anything about it. I don't see why I should get into trouble just because you want to go to a stupid concert.'

'You won't have to do anything except let me in afterwards,' Amanda said. 'I'd deal with everything else.'

'And remember you promised to do half the work with Quasimodo,' I reminded her.

'With *what*?' Amanda said.

'Quasimodo,' I said. 'That's the name of the puppy I've decided I'm going to have.'

'You can't call a puppy Quasi – what was it?'

'Modo.'

'Quasimodo!' Amanda said, shaking her head. 'Which one of your weird friends thought that up? Fern, I bet. She's the nerdiest one of the whole bunch of you.'

121

'You really think it's a dumb name?' I said.

'It's horrible!' Amanda said.

I nodded. 'I kind of thought that, too, but we chose the names between us, so there wasn't a whole lot I could do about it. I guess I'll change it once he moves in.'

'You could call him Eddie,' Amanda said. 'That's a nice name.'

'I'll get back to you on that,' I said. Quasimodo might be a weird name, but I wasn't about to let Amanda call the poor thing Eddie. I'd rather go back to the name Cindy came up with: Paddle-steamer.

Well, thinking up a new name for him was just the start! As soon as Mom and Dad were ready to let me know I could have a puppy, I'd have a whole load of things to think about. I just hoped they'd tell me *soon*. It was going to be real difficult if I had to pretend I didn't know for more than a couple of days.

Of course, if I thought *that* was going to be difficult, that was only because I didn't realise what was coming up over the weekend.

Chapter Twelve

I met Fern by our lockers on Friday morning.

'Have you had any response to the posters?' I asked.

Fern showed me her crossed fingers. 'Not yet,' she said.

The posters had been up around the neighbourhood for a couple of days now. I guess we were all worried that Hobo's owner would see one of the posters and turn up to claim Hobo and the puppies.

'My folks are going to let me have a puppy after all,' I told Fern.

'That's great,' Fern said. 'How come your mom changed her mind?'

'I don't know,' I said. I told her what I'd heard.

'And you're sure they were talking about a puppy?' Fern asked.

'What else *could* they have been talking about?' I said.

Pippa came running up. 'Has anyone called you about – '

'No!' Fern and I chorused.

'Phew!' Pippa breathed. 'That's two whole days. I think we're going to be in luck.'

'I feel kind of sorry for the people who lost her, though,' Fern said.

'That's true,' Pippa said. 'I'm kind of hoping they weren't very nice people.' She grinned. 'That way we don't have to feel bad about them.'

I guess that was more or less how I felt about it, too.

'Stacy's mom is letting her have a puppy after all,' Fern said.

'Really?' Pippa said. 'I thought she was dead set against it.'

'So did I,' I said. 'But she's changed her mind.' I looked at Fern. 'Can I choose which one I want?'

'Of course,' Fern said.

'I like Quasimodo best,' I said. 'He's the most adventurous one.'

'Yeah,' Fern said. 'He's my favourite, too.'

'Except for the *name*,' Pippa said. 'That *has* to be the worst dog name I've ever heard!'

'You don't like it?' Fern said. 'I thought it was . . . kind of . . . *unique*. How many dogs are there around called Quasimodo?'

'None,' I said. 'And doesn't that *tell* you something? I mean, if Quasimodo was such a neat name for a dog, how come no one else ever thought so?'

'Most people don't have my imagination,' Fern said.

'You can say that again,' Pippa said.

'OK, OK,' Fern said. 'If you don't like the name, we can change it.'

'We could each choose a name,' Pippa said. 'Including Cindy, of course. And then we can vote on which name we like best, except that we can't vote for our own name.'

'That sounds OK,' Fern said. 'Let me think. I've got to come up with something amazing. How about Archibald? Archibald's a pretty impressive name, don't you think, guys? Guys?' Pippa and I headed off down the corridor. 'Don't walk off while I'm talking to you! Hey! OK, not Archibald. How about Manhattan? No, wait! Philadelphia! Then you could call him Phil for short.'

Oh, boy. If Fern got her way, that poor dog was going to have the weirdest name ever.

'Did you sort everything out with Cheryl?' I asked Amanda as we got off the school bus and headed home that afternoon.

'Sure,' Amanda said. 'No problems. We're going to meet at seven-fifteen tomorrow night.'

'You'd better hope dinner is on time,' I said.

'It will be,' Amanda said determinedly. 'Even if I have to cook it myself! And then . . .' she let out a big wistful sigh, 'This Way To Paradise!'

'So Cheryl's going to pretend to go to bed early, too, is she?' I asked.

'She hasn't decided how she's going to play it,' Amanda said. 'She'll think of something.'

'I don't want to depress you,' I said, 'but if I was planning something like this, the last person I'd want to do it with would be Cheryl Ruddick.'

'Cheryl's OK,' Amanda said. 'I don't know why you don't like her. At least she's fun to be with. Unlike the oddballs *you* go around with.'

'Excuse me!' I said. 'Your friends aren't going to win any personality awards. Face it, Amanda, anyone with a friend like Rachel

Goldstein is in a pretty poor position to make fun of anyone else's friends.'

'Rachel can't help being kind of slow,' Amanda said. 'My friends are really OK if you'd only take the effort to get to know them.'

'They call me a nerd,' I said. 'Why should I want to spend time getting to know people who think I'm a nerd? And before you answer that, remember that it's me who's going to have the final say over whether you get to sleep in your own bed tomorrow night.'

'They think you're a nerd because they don't know you like I do.' Amanda said with a big sickly smile. 'You're not nearly as nerdish as you look, honestly!'

'Oh, right! So I'm not really a nerd. I just *look* like one! Is that what you're saying?'

'No, no,' Amanda said. 'I meant that even if you *did* look like a nerd, you wouldn't be. But you don't anyway, so there's no problem – is there?'

'I'd quit while I was ahead if I were you,' I said, as we walked up the driveway to our house. 'And, whatever you say, I still wouldn't want to have to rely on Cheryl for everything to go right tomorrow night.'

'Shh!' Amanda hissed as she opened the door. 'Don't *talk* about it here!'

* * *

Something else that wasn't talked about that evening was my puppy. I couldn't understand why Mom and Dad didn't just come right out and tell me I could have one. What were they waiting for?

I gave them plenty of opportunities. Like helping to clear up Sam's toys and accidentally pressing the puppy button on his yellow box.

'P is for puppy,' said the electronic voice. I gave Dad a hopeful look. Nothing!

I left Pippa's dog book on the kitchen table then went in there while Mom was fixing supper.

'Have you seen my dog book?' I asked.

'It's on the table,' Mom said.

'Oh, so it is,' I said. 'I could leave it for you, if you'd like to take a look at it.'

'No thanks, honey,' Mom said.

See what I mean? There I was, giving them plenty of chances to tell me that I *could* have a puppy after all, and they just weren't taking any notice!

* * *

'We're going to the mall this morning, if any-one's interested,' Dad said over breakfast the next morning. 'Amanda? Do you want to come?'

'No thanks,' Amanda said. 'I'm kind of busy today.'

'I'll come with you,' I said. 'Are you going for anything special?'

'Sam needs some new clothes,' Mom said. 'But apart from that, we're just going to do some window-shopping – maybe have lunch over there. You sure you don't want to come, Amanda?'

'Huh? Oh, no thanks. I've got to go and check something out with Cheryl,' she said.

Yeah, and I knew what. Tonight was *the night*.

'Oh, yes,' Mom said. 'Are you going to sleep over at her house tonight?'

'No,' Amanda said. 'I kind of changed my mind. Maybe some other time.'

'Oh, fine,' Mom said. I don't know if it was my imagination, but I could have sworn that Mom sounded relieved. Maybe she'd decided Cheryl was a bad influence. (I could have told her *that* three years ago!)

Not that I spent a whole lot of time trying to figure it out. I had enough to do, keeping Sam entertained in the back of the car as we drove across to the Clearwater Mall.

There is one store I really like to spend some time in whenever I go to the mall. It's called Pet Paradise.

I usually go in there to see Tonton. Tonton is a big red macaw who sits on a branch in the middle of the store, cracking nuts with his beak.

They don't only have birds for sale in Pet Paradise. They sell everything you could possibly think of. Fish and reptiles and birds and hamsters and kittens and puppies. Everything! And the animals are really well looked after. Sometimes I chat to the girls who work in there on Saturday.

I wish I was old enough to have a Saturday job! I'd love to work in Pet Paradise.

I was pretty patient as we wandered around the mall. I mean, I didn't just grab Sam's baby buggy and go zooming off to Pet Paradise. But I did do my best to lead Mom and Dad in that direction. I thought that maybe it would be the perfect opportunity for letting them know I'd overheard them the other night. I mean, while we were *there* we might as well buy some of the stuff the new puppy was going to need.

'Can we take a look in Pet Paradise?' I asked.

'Sure,' Mom said. 'So long as you're not planning on buying any more toys for Benjamin. I'm forever tripping over plastic mice and furry caterpillars as it is.'

I grinned at her. 'I wasn't thinking of buying anything for Benjamin,' I said. 'But I thought we might be needing some *other* stuff pretty soon.'

Mom looked blankly at me.

'You can tell me,' I said, looking from Mom to Dad. 'You don't need to keep it a secret any more.'

Dad shook his head. 'I'm sorry, honey. What are you talking about?'

'The puppy,' I said.

'Now, come on, Stacy,' Mom said. 'I thought we'd settled this. We *can't* have a puppy. It's just not practical right now.'

My big grin faded a little. 'It won't *be* right now,' I said. 'It won't be for another six weeks or so. The puppies have to be weaned first.'

'Six weeks doesn't make any difference, Stacy,' Mom said. 'When I said *right now*, I meant for the forseeable future. I just don't have the time to look after a puppy on top of everything else I have to do.'

'Amanda and I would look after it,' I said.

'You'll both be at school all day,' Mom

said. 'I don't have the time or the energy to run around after a puppy, Stacy. Now, let's not argue about this. We're not having a puppy, and that's the end of the story.'

'Your mom's right, sweetheart,' Dad said. 'Maybe in a few years' time we can think about having a dog.'

I was too stunned to say a word. I could hardly believe what I was hearing. I'd been so *sure* that they'd been talking about letting me have a puppy the other night.

But even as I was trying to cope with the disappointment without bursting into tears right in the middle of the mall, a small voice in my head was asking a very particular question.

If Mom and Dad hadn't been talking about surprising me with a puppy – what had they been talking about?

Chapter Thirteen

My grandma has this motto kind of thing that she says when things go wrong. She says, 'Count your blessings'.

The idea is that, when you have a major disappointment, you're supposed to cheer yourself up by listing all the things that have gone right for you in the past.

It was worth a try.

Things That Have Gone Right
1. I've got Benjamin.
2. We've all got Sam.
3. I've got some really good friends.
4. Mom doesn't make me eat lima beans any more.

And while I was making lists, I decided to make one for things that have gone wrong. Like, counting your *problems*!

Things That Have Gone Wrong

1. I have to wear a brace on my teeth for the next couple of years.
2. I'm too skinny.
3. My face looks like an explosion in a freckle factory.
4. I'm not getting a puppy after all.

Hmm. That's four points on either side. *That* didn't make me feel a whole lot better.

I did my very best to be brave over lunch in the mall, but Mom and Dad must have seen I was pretty down.

'Stacy,' Dad said, holding my hand and giving me a sympathetic smile. 'You've got to understand, we're not doing this to upset you. We've thought about it long and hard. Don't you think your mom's got enough on her plate right now, without having a puppy to look after?'

'Yeah,' I sighed. 'I guess so.' I gave them a bleak smile. 'It's OK,' I said. 'At least I don't have to eat lima beans.'

'I beg your pardon?' Mom said.

'I'm looking on the bright side,' I said. 'Can I go see Fern this afternoon?'

'Sure you can, honey.' Dad said. 'We'll drop you off on the way home.'

Seeing that I wasn't going to have Quasimodo for my very own, I wanted to spend as much time with him as possible before he went off to his new home.

Wherever that was going to be. And one thing was for sure – I was going to make certain Quasimodo went to a *good* home.

Mrs Kipsak answered the door.

'Hi,' I said. 'Is Fern home?'

'She's in her room,' Mrs Kipsak said. 'I'm glad you're here, Stacy. Maybe you can help cheer her up.'

'Why? What's happened?' A lump came into my throat. 'The puppies are OK, aren't they?'

'They're fine,' Mrs Kipsak said. 'You go talk to Fern – she'll tell you all about it.'

I can't remember the last time I saw Fern crying. I mean, she just doesn't do things like that. But she was crying now. She was sitting on the floor in the corner of her room, with her arms wrapped round a pillow and her face streaming with tears.

'Fern! What's happened!' I said, running over and putting my arms around her.

'Stupid darn posters!' Fern snuffled. 'Some stupid person saw our lost dog posters. They recognised the description.'

'Oh, no!' I said. 'Have they taken Hobo?'

135

'She's not called Hobo,' Fern said, wiping the back of her hand over her eyes. 'She's called Sapphire.'

'What happened?' I asked. 'Did they just turn up here and take her away?'

'No. Mom persuaded them to let her stay here for a few weeks, until the puppies are a bit bigger.'

I sat down next to Fern on the floor. Apart from the odd sniff from Fern, we just sat there in silence for a while.

'My folks weren't going to let me have a puppy after all,' I said. 'I got it all wrong.' I gave a big sigh. 'Did Hobo's owners seem nice people?'

Fern snuffled. 'Yeah, I guess so,' she said. 'They're called the Burtons. There are three little kids: Josie, Peter and Lorraine. They're five, six and seven.' Fern wiped her eyes with her sleeve and looked at me. 'You should have seen their faces when they saw Ho -, I mean, Sapphire and her pups! Their Dad said they'd been really miserable ever since Sapphire went missing. They live over near Roseway.'

'Wow,' I said. 'So Hobo – Sapphire, I mean – must have walked a couple of miles at least.'

'That's right,' Fern said. 'The littlest kid, Peter, left the back gate open, and no one realized that Sapphire was gone until the next morning.'

'At least we get to keep Sapphire for a few weeks,' I said.

'Yeah, I know,' Fern said. 'And Mr Burton said I can have one of the puppies for having looked after Sapphire so well.'

'Quasimodo!' I said.

'Yeah, except I don't think we should call him that any more. I think we should call him Lucky.' Fern smiled at me. 'Mom says it's OK for me to keep him. But he's not going to be *my* dog. He's going to belong to all of us, right? You, me, Cindy and Pippa. He'll be *our* dog.'

Our dog, Lucky.

Now that's what I call a happy ending!

* * *

Except that I guess you'd like to know what happened with Amanda and the Eddie Eden concert that night.

I spent the rest of the afternoon at Fern's house. Fern called Cindy and Pippa, and all four of us made a big fuss of Hobo-Sapphire, it was sad to think she'd be taken away, but it was really exciting to know that we'd be able to keep Lucky.

We all agreed that Lucky was a brilliant name, although Pippa said we should give him a proper Kennel Club type name as well. (OK, so Lucky was just a mongrel – but that doesn't mean he can't have a classy name.) Which is how come he ended up being called Lucky Quasimodo Paddle-steamer Hawkeye Lafayette Kipsak-Spiegel-Allen-Kane the First!

I got home round dinner time.

'Careful, Amanda,' I heard Mom say from the kitchen. 'It's not a *race*, you know.'

'But I'm hungry,' I heard Amanda say. 'Can't you speed it up a little?'

I went through to the kitchen. I could smell goulash. Mom was busy cooking, and Amanda was buzzing around her like a mad fly. I looked at the wall clock. It was a quarter-past six. If Amanda's plan was going to work, she had to be out of the house in three-quarters of an hour.

'I'll set the table,' Amanda said. 'How long's it going to be?'

'As long as it takes,' Mom said. 'What *is* it with you tonight, girl? Have you got ants in your pants?'

'I just want to have dinner and then get on with that art project I told you about,' Amanda said. Aha! So Amanda had used my idea. (I thought she would. If she'd decided to wait for an idea of her own to come along, she wouldn't have got out before Christmas.)

I told Mom about Sapphire, and about us keeping Lucky as our jointly owned dog.

'That's just perfect,' Mom said. 'So now everyone's happy!' Amanda barged up against her as she tried to get at the cutlery drawer. 'Except for your sister, who seems to have snipers in her diapers this evening. Amanda, for the last time, get out from under my feet!'

'Huh!' Amanda groaned. 'That's the last time I put myself out to help around this house. Talk about not being appreciated.'

'I do appreciate you, sweetie,' Mom said. 'But I'd appreciate you even more if you'd go and be helpful somewhere else.'

It was a pretty close-run thing. Mom called out that dinner was ready at half-past six.

'Woah!' Dad said, as Amanda started shovelling goulash down herself. 'Steady on, Amanda. You'll choke yourself!'

'*Umph, umgle gumph*,' Amanda said.

'It's OK,' I said. 'We were shown the Heimlich manoeuvre in a first-aid film at school. I'd like the chance to practise it on someone.' The Heimlich manoeuvre is this special *thing* you do to help people out when they're choking on food.

Amanda did some frantic chewing and swallowing. 'Sorry,' she said. 'I'm hungry. Mmm. This is really nice, Mom.'

'I'm surprised you can taste it,' Mom said. 'It's going down so fast I'll bet it's not even touching your tongue.'

'I want to put in a good night's work on my project,' Amanda said. 'And I don't want to be disturbed, OK! I'm going to need complete peace and quiet.'

'What exactly is this project?' Dad asked.

Amanda took a whole mouthful of food. I could see by her expression that she hadn't expected that question. She was obviously hoping that inspiration would hit her while she was emptying her mouth.

'It's a surprise,' I said. 'She's not telling anyone what it is until it's finished. Isn't that right, Amanda?'

'*Muggm mugy*,' Amanda said, nodding.

'Oh, good,' Mom said. 'I like surprises.'

Don't bet on it, Mom. I don't think you'd like this particular surprise if you found out what it was.

'May I be excused?' Amanda asked, at about two minutes to seven.

'Don't you want any dessert?' Mom said. 'It's your favourite. Chocolate cake and ice cream.'

'No, that's OK,' Amanda said as she got up. 'I don't want to eat too much, or I'll be too full to want to work.' She went to the door. 'I don't want to be disturbed at all tonight,' she said. 'No matter *what*!'

'No one will disturb you,' Mom said.

Amanda went clumping upstairs. Mom cut three slices of cake.

'She doesn't know what she's missing,' Dad said as Mom scooped out the ice cream.

While I was eating my slice of cake, I heard a creak on the stairs: Amanda creeping back down. I had my head down, but I glanced at Mom and Dad. They didn't seem to have heard anything. *I* must only have heard it because I was listening so hard.

There was a faint *snick* sound from the front hall: the sound of Amanda quietly closing the front door behind her. *Oh well*, I thought, *that's it! She's done it now.*

'This cake is delicious,' Dad said.

'Why, thanks,' Mom said. 'I bought the whole thing myself.'

'Amanda won't have started work yet,' Dad said. 'I'll take her up a little slice.'

141

'She said she didn't want any,' I said.

'I know,' Dad said. 'But one tiny slice isn't going to hurt her.'

I jumped up out of my seat. 'I'll take it to her,' I said.

'Oh, OK,' Dad said. He cut her a narrow slice of cake and plopped a scoopful of ice cream next to it. 'With the compliments of the chef,' he said, as I took the plate from him.

I went upstairs and knocked on Amanda's bedroom door.

'Amanda, can I come in? I've got some cake for you, Dad says one little slice won't do you any harm.'

I opened the door.

Well! Surprise, surprise! Amanda *wasn't there*!

'Yes, I know,' I said loudly as I went into the room. 'I'll tell them you don't want to be disturbed for anything else all night.' I put the plate on her desk and went back downstairs. (But I ate the ice cream myself.)

We cleared the table and Dad and I went into the living room to watch TV. A couple of minutes later, Mom came through to pick up some mugs and bowls that had been left in there earlier.

'Don't bother with that,' Dad said, patting the couch. 'Come and sit down.'

'I'll only be a couple of seconds,' Mom said. 'I'm just going to finish filling the dishwasher. Have you got any mugs or anything in your room, Stacy?'

'Nope, I don't think so,' I said.

'Well, I know your sister has,' Mom said. 'I'll just pop up there and get them.'

'But she doesn't want to be disturbed!' I said.

'I shan't disturb her,' Mom said. She started climbing the stairs.

Ohmygosh! Amanda had only been gone ten minutes and already Mom was about to discover that she was missing!

But what could I do about it?

Chapter Fourteen

'Maybe I do have some things in my room for the dishwasher,' I said, scrambling frantically over my dad on the couch. 'I'll just go and check.'

'I don't think it's *that* urgent,' Dad said as I zipped out into the hall. Mom was at the top of the stairs.

'Hey! Mom!' I called. I raced up the stairs and gave her a hug.

'What's brought this on?' Mom said, stroking my hair.

'You do so much work for us,' I said. 'You must be the busiest mom in the entire world. Let *me* sort out the stuff for the dishwasher, huh? You just go down and watch TV with Dad.'

'Well, aren't you a sweetheart,' Mom said with a big smile. 'But I'm here now.' She took a step toward Amanda's room. 'Stacy, you can let go now.'

'She'll be real mad if you disturb her,' I said.

'She won't even notice me,' Mom said, turning the handle of Amanda's door.

She opened the door. 'She's not in here,' Mom said.

Think! Come on, brain, don't let me down now.

'She must be in the bathroom,' I said. I ran to the bathroom door as Mom went into Amanda's room.

I rattled the handle. 'Oh!' I called. 'You *are* in there. OK, OK, I was only checking.' I stood in the doorway of Amanda's room. Mom was in there picking up mugs and dishes and plates.

'Your sister!' she said. 'Look at this. No wonder I can never find anything downstairs. Three mugs, two bowls and two plates. And she hasn't eaten her cake yet.' She came out into the hall. 'Amanda! You bring things downstairs in future, you hear me?'

She went downstairs. Phew! I'd gotten away with it!

I nipped into the bathroom and flushed the toilet. Then I did an Amanda-stomp across to her door and went inside, giving it a good Amanda-slam.

I devoured the slice of cake as quick as I

could, then came out of Amanda's room with the empty plate.

I ran downstairs and into the kitchen.

'Amanda said "Thanks, it was really good",' I told Mom, as I slid the plate and fork into the dishwasher.

'There's plenty more, if she wants it,' Mom said.

'No, she said she'd had enough,' I said.

'Do *you* know what this project is she's working on?' Mom asked.

'No-o,' I said. 'At least . . . I don't . . . I think . . . she said . . . um . . . it was . . . something . . . uh . . .'

'Stacy? Are you OK?' Mom asked. 'It was a simple enough question, surely? Either you know or you don't.'

'It's a secret,' I said. I slammed the dishwasher closed and turned the dial. I grabbed Mom's hand before she had the chance to come up with any other bright ideas that involved her having to go into Amanda's room.

'You've done enough for today,' I said, towing her along the hall and into the living room. 'You just sit there and watch TV.'

Peace at last! Mom stretched her legs out over Dad's lap while I sat on the floor, with my head resting against her side.

About half an hour later, Benjamin came strolling in and decided that he wanted petting by all of us. This involved him walking up me, onto Mom and then down Mom's legs to Dad, picking up strokes as he went.

He did this about five times before he finally started to settle himself in Mom's lap.

'For heaven's sake, cat!' she said. 'Will you just lie down.' I looked around, Benjamin is real fussy that his bed should be *purr-fect*, which means he had to walk round and round in these tight circles, pawing at Mom until she felt just right. Then and only then, could he lie down for a sleep.

'Is that rain?' Mom said, a few minutes later. Dad turned the sound on the TV down with the remote control and we all listened.

'It sure is,' Dad said. It sounded like quite a storm, by the way the rain was pattering against the window. There was a flash of light against the closed drapes.

I counted. 'One, two, three, four, five, six.' A rumble of thunder sounded. 'That means the storm is two miles away,' I said. 'Sound travels at one mile every three seconds.'

'I don't care where it is,' Dad said. 'We're all snug and dry in here.'

Two miles. I thought. Fairfield Hall is about

two miles away. And I know *one* member of this family who wasn't snug and dry at home.

Then I remembered something. Hadn't Amanda said she was going to bunch up pillows to make it look like she was in bed asleep if Mom or Dad went into her room later? There hadn't been any bunched-up pillows in her bed when *I'd* gone in there. She must have forgotten about it. (Which was pretty lucky, really, because Mom would have seen them when she went up to collect the crockery.)

I made a mental note to slide into her room and make up a sleeping-Amanda shape for her when I went up to bed later.

The thunder seemed to fade away pretty quickly, but the rain kept up all evening.

There was faint wail from upstairs. Sam had woken up.

Mom made as if to tip Benjamin off, but Dad got up. 'I'll go and see what the problem is,' he said.

'Thanks, honey,' Mom said.

I turned around on to my knees and gave Benjamin a pet. 'I guess a puppy dog *would* have been a lot of extra work.' I said, as Benjamin started purring in his sleep. 'And now that Fern is keeping one of the puppies, I'll get all the fun and none of the hard work.'

'That's right,' Mom said. 'That's just what your Grandma says about you, Sam and Amanda. She has all the fun of children without any of the down-side.'

'What's the down-side?' I asked.

'Oh, I don't know,' Mom said. 'When you and Amanda fight – that's a down-side.'

'We haven't fought for weeks,' I said.

'I know,' Mom said. 'And that's the up-side!'

'Can I ask you something?' I said. 'What were you and Dad talking about the other night? I wasn't listening on purpose, but I heard you say something about a surprise. You said it was hard to keep it a secret, and Dad said it would be worth it to see *her* face when she found out. What were you talking about?'

Before Mom said anything, Dad came back.

'Sam's gone back to sleep,' he said, lifting Mom's legs and sliding in under them on the couch. 'He wasn't really awake at all.'

'Stacy heard us talking about the big secret the other night,' Mom said to Dad. 'Should we tell her?'

'I guess we can,' Dad said. 'We were going to tell them both in the morning, anyway. I'll call Amanda so we can tell them together?'

'Tell us what?' I asked. 'What is it?'

Mom and Dad were both grinning.

'You know your sister has been on and on at us about going to see Eddie Eden?' Dad said.

I nodded blankly. 'Yeah.'

'You like Eddie Eden, too, don't you?' Mom said.

'Sure,' I said. 'I mean, I'm not *crazy* about him the way Amanda is, but I like his music.'

'We've bought tickets for the two of you for tomorrow night's concert in Mayville,' Mom said with a big smile. 'We're going to drive you over there for the concert. Then your Dad and I are going to have a romantic candlelit dinner for two at a really swanky restaurant. And then we'll pick you up afterward and bring you back.'

'We bought the tickets weeks ago,' Dad said. 'But we wanted it to be a big surprise for the two of you.' He laughed. 'And believe me, keeping it from Amanda all this time has been a real effort!'

Mom looked at me. 'You don't seem too excited about it,' she said. 'I thought you'd *want* to go with Amanda.'

'Oh, yes!' I gasped. 'I don't know what to say. It's such a surprise!' Sheesh! You can say that again, Stacy. The word 'surprise' didn't even come close!

'That's why I didn't really want Amanda staying over at Cheryl's house tonight,' Mom said. 'You'll both be having a late night tomorrow, without Amanda staying up chatting to Cheryl all night tonight.'

'But you told her she was too young to go to a rock concert,' I said.

'She's certainly too young to go to one all by herself,' Dad said. 'But, like we said, we'll take you there and pick you up afterwards.'

'Why didn't you get tickets for the concert in Four Corners?' I asked. 'Why drive all the way to Mayville?'

'Because all the really good tickets were sold out for the Fairfield Hall concert,' Mom said. 'But we managed to get you tickets for the hall in Mayville right at the front.'

'Is that a neat surprise, or what?' Dad said with a grin. 'I can't wait to see Amanda's face when we tell her. She'll go ape!' He lifted Mom's legs up out of his lap and got off the couch.

'In fact,' he said. 'I'm not going to wait. I'm going to tell her right now!'

'She doesn't want to be disturbed!' I almost shrieked.

'You're kidding,' Dad said with a big smile. 'She won't mind being disturbed by *this*!'

'Da-ad!'

But it was too late. He was running up the stairs.

'What's wrong, honey?' Mom asked, looking at me. 'You look a little pale.'

I gave her a weak smile. 'Do you really, really love Amanda and me?' I asked.

'Sure, I do,' Mom said.

'And will you always love us, no matter what we do?' I asked.

'Of course.'

I took hold of her hand. 'Promise?'

Mom smiled. 'I promise. What is this. Stacy? What on earth's the matter?'

I heard Dad come running down the stairs.

'Remember,' I said, looking into my mom's puzzled face. 'You promised!'

Dad came into the living room.

'She's not there,' he said. 'There's no sign of her.'

They both looked at me.

'Stacy!' Mom growled. 'Where is your sister?'

I gave them an anxious look and a hopeful kind of smile. 'I can explain,' I said. 'Honest. I *can* explain.'

152

Chapter Fifteen

'Of all the stupid, thoughtless, irresponsible, harebrained ideas!' Mom exploded, after I'd finished my explanation.

I kind of got the feeling that she wasn't too pleased.

I was sitting in the middle of the couch, feeling about two inches big while Mom wore out the rug in front of me, pacing up and down.

'And you helped her!' Mom said angrily. 'You're supposed to be the intelligent one in this family. Don't you realize the kind of things that can happen to a thirteen-year-old girl out on her own at this time of night?'

'She's with Cheryl,' I mumbled.

'Huh, *Cheryl*!' Mom said. 'Why did you let her do it?'

'What could I do?' I said unhappily.

'You could have stopped her!' Mom yelled.

'How?' I moaned. 'She's bigger than me.' I

felt shivery inside. It wasn't because Mom was angry – it was because I could see that she was very worried.

'And she's just gone there with Cheryl?' Dad asked, leaning on the back of the couch behind me.

I corkscrewed my head around and looked up at him. 'Uh-huh,' I said.

'And Cheryl's mom doesn't know anything about this either?' he asked.

I shook my head. I had a tight feeling in my throat and the backs of my eyes felt all hot and prickly.

'*Anything* could happen to them out there,' Mom said. 'The stupid girls!'

'I think the first thing to do is call Cheryl's mom,' Dad said. He looked at me. 'Did Amanda say what time the concert was due to finish?'

'Late.' I said. 'I don't know exactly what time. Amanda was going to throw stones at my window when she got back, and I was going to let her in the back way.' I tried to swallow the lump in my throat.

'The concert in Mayville was going to end at ten o'clock,' Mom said. 'I guess this one will end around the same time.'

Dad looked at his watch. It was ten past nine.

'I can drive over there and pick them up,' Dad said. 'There's only one bus route through here, so I know where they'll be waiting.'

'OK,' Mom said. 'And I'll call Anna Ruddick.'

I looked at them. I was feeling so bad you wouldn't believe it: not because they were mad at Amanda for sneaking out or mad at me for helping her, but because they were so obviously worried sick about her.

I guess that was the first time I'd actually *thought* about why they didn't want Amanda to go to the concert on her own.

They went out into the hall. I followed them and stood in the doorway.

Dad put on his coat while Mom searched the pin-board for Cheryl's phone number.

'She'll be OK, won't she?' I asked. My voice sounded real trembly.

'Of course she will,' Dad said.

I felt a couple of hot tears running down my face. 'So why are you so worried?' I said. 'What do you think has happened to her?'

'Nothing,' Mom said, reaching out and taking hold of my wrist. She towed me towards her and put her arm around my waist to give me a squeeze. 'We don't think anything's happened, Stacy.'

'It's all my fault!' I said. 'I gave her the idea of sneaking out. I told her to say she was doing a project in her room.' I sniffed back some tears. 'She wouldn't have been able to go if I hadn't agreed to let her back in. It's *all* my fault!'

Dad patted my head. 'Don't worry,' he said. 'Nothing's going to happen to her.'

'Not until you get her back here, anyway,' Mom said. 'Where the heck is Cheryl's phone number?'

'Amanda must have it in her room,' I said. 'Do you want me to go and get it?'

'Yes, please, Stacy,' Mom said. 'And – '

Ding-dong!

Ding-dong! Ding-dong! The doorbell rang urgently.

Dad opened the door.

'Amanda!' Mom yelled.

I stared at the bedraggled figure in the porch. It *looked* like Amanda, although it could have been a drowned rat. There was a policewoman with her. Behind them, the rain was still falling hard.

'We found this young lady outside Fairfield Hall,' said the policewoman.

Amanda gave the weediest of weedy smiles. 'Hi, Mom. Hi, Dad,' she said, as the rain ran down her straggly, flattened hair and over her face. She looked like someone had just thrown a bucket of water over her. She was totally soaked! I've seen drier looking things sitting at the bottom of aquariums.

'Apparently, she was expecting to meet a friend,' the policewoman said. 'But her friend never turned up.'

Amanda stepped over the threshold and stood dripping in the hall.

'I'm wet,' she said, 'and I'm cold. And I never even got to the concert!' She threw herself at Dad and burst into tears.

★　★　★

We were in the kitchen. Amanda was wrapped in bath towels and Mom was rubbing her hair with a hand towel. We were all having a mug of hot chocolate while Amanda explained what had happened.

'I waited for Cheryl for a half-hour,' Amanda said, her voice all wobbly because Mom was shaking her head around so much while she rubbed her hair dry.

'And then it got to around a quarter to eight,' Amanda continued. 'I thought maybe

I'd made a mistake. I thought maybe Cheryl was expecting to meet up with me outside the Hall. So I went there.' *Rub rub rub* went Mom's hands, *shake shake shake* went Amanda's head.

'But she wasn't there,' Amanda said. 'And it was raining. And the big bully doormen wouldn't let me in because I didn't have a ticket. And I got *soaked*. And Cheryl still didn't turn up!' She began to sniff again. 'And then the concert started and I was just left *standing* there in the pouring rain.'

'Why didn't you tell the doormen what had happened?' asked Dad.

'I did,' Amanda said. 'But they didn't believe me. They thought I was trying to get into the concert without a ticket. And I started yelling at them and telling them what a bunch of dumb jerks they were. And then a police car came along, and the policewoman asked "where my parents were?" And I said, "They're at home." And she said, "Get in, we're taking you home." '

Amanda's voice broke into a wail. 'And here I am! And I didn't get to see Eddie Eden, and I don't know what happened to Cheryl, and I'm so miserable I just want to die!' She grabbed a handful of towel and wiped her bright red nose.

'And now I'm going to get punished worse than I've ever been punished in my *life*!' she howled. 'And all for nothing!'

'Calm down,' Mom said. 'The first thing we've got to find out is what happened to Cheryl. How come she didn't meet you at the bus-stop?'

'I don't know,' Amanda moaned.

'So call her,' Mom said. 'Call her *now*!' Dad got up from the table and brought the phone in from the hall.

Amanda pressed out Cheryl's number. She had time to wipe her nose again before anyone answered.

'Oh, hi, Mrs Ruddick,' Amanda said. 'It's Amanda. I'm sorry I'm calling so late, but is Cheryl there?' There was a pause, then Amanda said. 'Oh, great. Yes, please, if you could.'

Amanda had been using her ultra-polite voice on Mrs Ruddick, but she sounded like a rabid Rottweiler when Cheryl came on the other end of the line.

'Where the heck *were* you?' she howled into the receiver. 'I stood there waiting for you for half an hour. I got totally soaked. I got picked up by the police!'

I could faintly hear Cheryl's voice whining down the phone.

'That's *pathetic*!' Amanda yelled. 'I'm not talking to you *ever again*, Cheryl Ruddick. Goodbye.'

Whack! She slammed the phone down.

'So what was the answer?' Mom asked.

'She couldn't think of a way to get out of the house without her mom knowing,' Amanda said. 'Her mom wanted to call here to make sure it was OK for her to sleep over. So she had to give up on that idea, and she couldn't think of any other way of getting out! She said she was really sorry. *Really* sorry! Sheesh!'

'At least we know she's safe,' Dad said. He frowned at Amanda. 'And at least *you*'re safe,' he said. 'Do you realise how dangerous it could have been for you out there at this time of night?'

'Yes, I do. Honestly, I do *now*. But I really wanted to see the concert,' Amanda said with a sniffle. 'And you wouldn't let me go. You just don't understand. You don't understand how much it meant to me. And now I've missed my only chance ever in my entire life to see Eddie Eden. And on top of that you're going to ground me for the next twenty billion years, *and* take me off the cheerleading squad, probably, and stop me being friends with Cheryl and . . . and . . . everything bad in the *world*!'

'Don't you think you deserve to be punished?' Mom asked.

'I guess I do,' Amanda said. 'But Stacy shouldn't be punished. It wasn't her fault. She was just helping me out.'

'We'll have to think about that,' Mom said. She wrapped her arms around Amanda's neck. 'But what are we going to do with *you*, young lady? That's the question.'

'What would you do if you were in our position?' Dad asked.

'Ground me for . . . uh . . . a month?' Amanda said.

Mom and Dad looked at each other.

'And do you think that'll teach you not to tell us fibs and not to go sneaking out of the house without letting us know what you're doing?' Dad said.

Amanda nodded. 'It sure would,' she said.

'OK, then,' Dad said. 'You're grounded for four weeks. Starting Monday night.'

'*Monday* night?' Amanda asked. 'Why *Monday* night?'

Mom unwrapped her arms from around Amanda's neck and went over to her shoulder-bag that was hanging behind the door.

'Because the rest of us are going out tomorrow night,' Mom said. 'And we can't leave you in the house all on your own. So I guess you're going to *have* to come with us.'

Amanda looked totally confused.

'Where are you *go-o-o-ooooohhhhooow-ow-ow-ow-ow-Wow! Wow! Wahhh*!' Mom laid the two tickets to the Mayville concert on the table in front of Amanda.

We all laughed as Amanda's voice rose to a shriek like a police siren and her eyes nearly popped out of her head.

'You. I. But. What? When? How . . .?' Amanda gabbled as she stared at the tickets in total disbelief.

'It's a miracle.' Dad laughed. 'Amanda is actually *speechless*!'

And he was right. For once in her life, my big sister couldn't think of a single thing to say.

And I guess that's the end of the story really, except to tell you that we had a fabulous time at the concert in Mayville. Oh, and I guess I ought to mention that I've got a couple of Eddie Eden posters up on my wall now, although I'm never, ever, *ever* going to be as big an Eddie Eden fan as Amanda.

And we even got to see Eddie at the stage door after the performance. (Us and about two zillion others!) I kept out of the way, but Amanda ploughed all the way to the front and got Eddie to autograph the concert program.

So now Amanda's got a *real* Eddie Eden autograph! I wonder whether I should tell her that the one *I* got for her is a fake. I think I probably *will* tell her . . . in a couple of *years*, maybe.

Oh, and one other thing. Lucky's full kennel name is now: Lucky *Eddie* Quasimodo Paddle-steamer Hawkeye Lafayette Kipsak-Spiegel-Allen-Kane the First.

Which, as Pippa pointed out, is a pretty big name for a dog you can put in your jacket pocket! But I guess he'll grow into it.

LITTLE SISTER
Book 6

Preview

Stacy and Amanda are back in **Little Sister Book 6**, *Sister Switch*, published by Red Fox. Here's a sneak preview:

Chapter One

RRRRRRIIIIINNNNNNGGGGGGGGGG!

Have you ever seen an entire class jump two feet into the air? Until that alarm clock went off it had been totally quiet in our classroom. The only sound you could hear was the scratching of pens on paper and the occasional groan as someone got to a question straight out of their nightmares.

'What on earth is going on?' Ms Fenwick bounded up out of her seat as though it had suddenly bitten her.

'Ow! Owowowowow!' Betsy Jane Garside was sitting right in front of me, and she started howling in pain because she'd jabbed her pencil in her eye when the alarm clock had gone off.

We were in the middle of a maths test. I was on Question Twelve. These two guys were travelling towards each other on trains. One of them had left Town A at six o'clock in the morning and was travelling east at eighty five miles an hour. The other guy had left town B at eight o'clock and was going west at seventy miles an hour. The towns were five hundred miles apart and we were supposed to figure out where and when the two guys would meet. If you ask me, they could have saved everyone a whole lot of trouble if they'd just *called* each other on the phone.

I was sitting there with my pencil in my mouth, gazing out of the window and imagining these two trains charging towards each other. But the question didn't mention whether they were on the same track. If they *were* on the same track, then I was thinking that the question should really read, 'Where and at what time will the two trains crash into each other?'

I guess you're not supposed to wonder about stuff like that in the middle of a maths test.

'It's a fire drill!' Larry Franco shouted. 'We should evacuate the building!'

'It's not a fire drill,' Ms Fenwick said. She came swooping up the aisle where I was sitting and homed in on my bag.

RRRRRRIIIIIIINNNNNNGGGGGG!

'Stacy, will you please put a stop to that infernal *noise*!' Ms Fenwick said.

That's me: Stacy Allen, once an ordinary ten year old student in Four Corners, Indiana. Now, the cause of infernal noises in the middle of maths tests.

'Betsy Jane, what were you yelling about?' Ms Fenwick asked.

'I jabbed my pencil in my eye!' Betsy Jane wailed.

While Ms Fenwick examined Betsy Jane's eye, I hauled my bag up onto my desk and rummaged through my stuff in search of the ringing alarm clock.

There it was. Right at the bottom. It got even louder as I pulled it out and jerked down the lever to shut it off.

'*Thank* you,' Ms Fenwick said. 'Quiet, everyone, please!'

The whole class was talking now and, out of Ms Fenwick's eyesight, a few kids were swapping answers.

Ms Fenwick's eagle-eyes moved around the class and everyone went quiet.

'Well, Stacy?' she said, looking at the alarm clock and then looking at me. 'Would you like to explain why you thought it was a good idea to bring an alarm clock to class?'

Good question.

But did I have a good answer? I sure did, but not one I could tell Ms Fenwick. I knew *exactly* how that alarm clock got into my bag. And it was nothing to do with me, I can tell you that. I *knew* who put it there, and I knew why.

'I must have put it in there by accident,' I said to Ms Fenwick. 'Things like that happen when you're in a hurry.' I added. I looked at my friend Cindy. 'Don't they?'

Cindy gave me a blank look for a second then nodded in agreement. 'They sure do,' she said. 'Last week I brought a tube of toothpaste into school by mistake. I don't know how it got in my bag, because I hadn't taken my bag into the bathroom at all that morning.'

'Aliens, I guess,' said Fern, who was sitting right behind us. Just recently Fern has started blaming aliens for anything strange that happens.

A tube of toothpaste appears in your school bag? Aliens!

An alarm clock goes off in the middle of a maths test? You got it: Aliens!

Bug-eyed monsters from Venus. Except that the bug-eyed monster who put the alarm clock in my bag wasn't from Venus. She was from the bedroom down the hall from mine. It was my big, airheaded bimbo of a sister, Amanda!

I knew *why*. It was her idea of a really great way of getting back at me for slipping one of Sam's dummies in with her cheerleading stuff the day before.

But I only did that to pay her back for pinning a *KICK ME* sign on to the back of my sweater the day before that. She *started* it!

Honest, she did! OK, so the *KICK ME* note was to get back at me for taking the laces out of her sneakers. But what would you do if your sister doctored your toothpaste with soap so you came screaming out of the bathroom foaming at the mouth like you had *rabies*?

I'll level with you. I don't really remember *who* started all this revenge stuff. But I was pretty determined about who was going to *finish* it.

Stacy Allen, that's who.

My first reaction was to hunt Amanda down after class and stuff the alarm clock right down her throat. But no; that wouldn't be *nearly* bad enough. What I needed to come up with was something so *sneaky*, so *diabolically* clever that people in our school would be talking about it in twenty years' time.

It would be known as *The Great Revenge*.

The day when Stacy finally won over her big sister! Brain over brawn. Not that Amanda's especially brawny, except between the ears.

Anyway, Ms Fenwick got everyone settled down again and we finished the maths test without anything going off in anyone else's bag. I guess no one else in my class has a crazy older sister like I do.

'Amanda's gone too far this time,' I told Fern, Cindy and Pippa as we headed back to my house after school. 'I'm going to have to *kill* her. It's the only way the rest of my life is going to be worth living.'

'I thought it was pretty funny,' Fern said with a grin, meaning Amanda's alarm-clock-in-the-bag routine. 'Did you see the way everyone jumped? Fern giggled. 'Things like that should happen more often.'

'Oh, right,' I said. 'I'll go tell Amanda to come up with more ways to make me look dumb in front of everyone. As long as *you* think it's funny!'

'Don't get upset,' Fern said. 'It *was* funny. You'd have thought it was funny if the clock had been in someone else's bag.'

'That's not the point,' I said. 'It wasn't in someone else's bag. It was in *my* bag. And Amanda has got to suffer for it!'

'It sure is an escalation,' Pippa said. Pippa's mom is a college professor. That's how come Pippa drops these long words into the conversation every once in a while.

We all looked at her.

'Doesn't that mean a hole in the ground?' Fern asked.

'No, that's an *excavation*,' Pippa said. 'An escalation is like when someone does something to someone else that's a lot worse than anything that the other person has already done to them in the first place.'

Cindy crossed her eyes and pulled a goofy face. 'Thanks for the explanation, Pippa,' she said. 'I understand *perfectly* now.'

'I think I get it,' I said. 'You mean, like I hide a baby's dummy in Amanda's stuff and she comes back with an alarm clock hidden in my bag and set to go off in the middle of a test.'

'Exactly,' Pippa said. 'That's escalation.'

'So Stacy has got to come up with something even *worse*,' Fern said. She gave me a thoughtful look. 'How about a bomb?'

'That's a great idea, Fern,' I said. 'Do you know anywhere I can get a bomb?'

'The bomb store in the mall?' Fern said.

'I *wish*!' I sighed. 'I wish there was a store full of useful stuff like that.'

That's exactly the kind of thing a younger sister like me needs. An Anti-Big-Sister Store. Not that Amanda and I are *always* fighting. But when we *do* fight it tends to *escalate* as Pippa would say.

And right now, it was me who had to come up with the perfect *escalation*.

'Oh, hi, Stacy.' I spun around. It was Amanda. She'd come up behind us without a sound. She grinned, lifting her arm and pushing her sleeve back to look at her watch.

'Oh, gee,' she said. 'My watch has stopped. Do you have any idea what time it is, Stacy?'

'Funn-ee!' I said. 'I think it's time you packed up and left town, because I'm going to get you but good!'

Amanda gave me this really surprised look.

'Why? What's wrong, Stacy? You look kind of *alarmed*.' She burst out laughing and then went running off to catch up with a bunch of her friends before I could think of anything to say back.

Ooh! Amanda Allen. I'm going to *get* you! I'm going to get you if it's the last thing I do!

174

At least, that was the plan until we all got back to my house and found a letter on the hall table that changed everything.